I0731397

THE SOLDIER'S MATE

THE BLUE SOLACE: BOOK THREE

C.W. GRAY

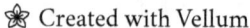 Created with Vellum

AUTHOR'S NOTE

The first half of Book Three in the Blue Solace series takes place about five months before the end of Book Two. The story begins with Dru and her crew on their mission to find and rescue Wyatt Morrick. The second half continues on from the end of Book Two.

The Blue Sparrow, en route to the Sugarworm System

"Sebastian says he's having a girl," Alois said, sitting sideways in his chair, legs hanging over one side and his head over the other. The Dedril looked pensive for a moment. "He's going to name her after his cousin Nina." His expression turned wistful as he talked about his maybe-mate. "He's taking on translation work for a lot of Leti's university colleagues. Sebastian still doesn't realize how smart he is. He'll be bringing in a nice, steady salary soon enough."

Morgan Murray leaned back in his chair, his long legs stretched out in front of him. "That's nice," he said. "Have you told him you already started a college fund for the baby?"

Alois blushed. "Of course not. He's a bit skittish, so

we're taking our time. I have to be cautious, so I don't scare him."

"You make him sound like a feral cat." Morgan brushed a strand of silky hair from his face and sipped his coffee.

He watched the two young women on the mats circle one another. When Quinn's chin dropped, Morgan raised his phaser and quickly zapped her in the shoulder. He had it set extremely low, but he knew it stung. She winced, then started moving again, without the chin drop.

"I just don't want to fuck up. Sebastian is special. I don't know for sure if he's my mate, but honestly, I don't give a damn. He's going to be mine."

"Aww," Morgan said. "That's so cute, the way you think it's your choice."

Quinn threw hit after hit, interspersed with the occasional kick, and Hazel blocked more than Morgan expected. The young engineer was getting better.

Hazel tapped her foot, readying a kick, and Morgan zapped her in the shin.

"Ouch," Hazel squeaked, then carried through on her kick, that time without the foot tap.

Quinn blocked it, then went on the offensive. The two got zapped three more times each before they finally collapsed on the mats.

"I still didn't get a fucking hit in," Hazel said. The young hybrid woman rubbed her pointed ears. Morgan had noticed she did that when she was stressed. Her light pink skin glistened in the light of the ship, and her white hair hung limply, wet with sweat. The poor thing looked pitiful.

"You're getting better, Hazel," Alois said, giving her an upside down smile from his chair. She smiled back, her grin infectious.

Quinn slowly rose to her feet. Morgan knew she had to be sore, but the woman sure as shit had some grit. He'd sparred with her himself that morning. She kept coming and coming, no matter how sore and tired she was. She would make a damn good fighter one day.

Right now, she was an average one, and average fighters died fast. He didn't want that for the tough hybrid woman. She had already suffered so much at the hands of the Concords.

"You both still have too many tells," Morgan said, standing smoothly. He paced around the women. "The expression on your face isn't the only thing your opponent sees. Quinn, you tilt your chin when you're about to attack, and your fingers twitch when you're about to throw a punch. Hazel, your face shows every emotion you feel."

Quinn groaned and dropped back to the mat, resting on her knees. "Any good news?"

"You're both getting better. Quinn, I only shot you four times. Hazel, you're down to eight. Yesterday, I shot you thirteen times. I know it's a pain in the ass to break these habits, but it's necessary."

"Let's do one more round, Hazel," Quinn said, voice hard. She stood and moved into position. "We have to be better if we want to stay alive long enough to help people."

"Okay," Hazel said, slowly getting to her feet. "One more round."

Morgan couldn't contain his proud grin. He had never wanted to be charged with training the crew – to make sure they were prepared to keep themselves alive and help others. It was a big responsibility, and he preferred being a simple soldier.

Then Hack and Dru had asked him to be the weapons specialist for the Blue Sparrow. Of course he had to agree. It was Hack and Dru. Now, he had three trainees and an ulcer.

Responsibility sucked. They were his fighters, though, getting ready to push through their pain to get better.

"Look at that proud papa grin," Alois said, fluttering his eyes. "Now who's cute?"

"Shut it," Morgan said, growling. He turned back to the women. "Get moving."

Their next match was much slower. They didn't focus on speed but on their tells. By the time Quinn had Hazel pinned to the mat, Morgan hadn't needed to shoot either of them.

"Much better," he said. "Slower, yeah, but better."

The women knelt on the mat, panting and smiling. "We'll get there," Hazel said.

"You will," Alois said, sitting up in his chair.

"Since you're making progress, we'll update your training a bit," Morgan said. "You'll both need to begin meditating. Plenty of people think it's a waste of time, but it will help you control your emotions."

Quinn whimpered. The woman definitely had

trouble staying still and quiet. Meditation would be hard for her.

"Meditating sounds better than sparring," Hazel said. The engineer-in-training had no problem with focus. She'd enjoy it.

"We're a week away from the Sugarworm System, so we'll get you both into a routine. First thing in the morning, you meditate right here for one hour, then do your normal amount of cardio. After breakfast, you two spar until Hazel has to go train with Lerais in engineering. Quinn, at that point, you'll start training with me, on the dummy, or with Linc, if he's available. Then, you both meditate for another hour before lunch. After lunch, we pick it up again until you both drop. Got it?"

"We can do it," Quinn said, nodding. Hazel nodded too, eyes starting to droop.

"Great. Go clean up and get some dinner. I'll see you both after breakfast tomorrow."

The two women walked stiffly from the training room, limping towards the hot showers.

Morgan watched them go, grinning. Quinn would be great by the time he was done with her. Hazel wasn't a natural fighter, she was an engineer, but her training was progressing faster than Selene and he had thought it would.

"You're doing damn good work, Morgan," Alois said, jumping to his feet. "Let's do a round. We need to stay in practice, so the trainees don't kick our asses."

They sparred, and Morgan knocked Alois on his ass. This time anyway. Alois shot him dirty looks as they both worked through their own routines. He did join in with Morgan for thirty minutes of meditation to finish the night.

Alois limped beside him. "When did you get so good? When did meditation become part of combat training?"

"I can't help it that I'm amazing, Alois. You slept too much during the last mission, so you missed out on my rise to glory."

"That's not how Draif described it. He said you got wounded again and again."

"Draif! What does he know?" Morgan grinned. He'd picked up meditation from Draif. The man had extensive combat training, but Alois didn't have to know that.

Alois gave him a suspicious look and headed toward his room.

Morgan went to his quarters to clean up.

His room on the Blue Sparrow was surprisingly just a little smaller than his space on the Blue Solace. It did have a nice-sized window, which was definitely better than the porthole he'd had before. He'd decorated in bold colors and crazy patterns. His walls were a deep blue, and a large abstract painting in purples and blues dominated one wall.

The hot water felt good on his tight muscles, and he hummed in pleasure as he showered. He used his favorite almond body wash and his special hair conditioner. After drying his hair and pampering himself, he dressed in soft, clean clothes and dropped into a chair.

He called Selene. She picked up quickly, her still, expressionless face comforting to see.

"Morgan," she said, voice as empty as her expression.

"If Dru asks you about shooting trainees with a phaser during training, just go with it, okay?"

"I don't shoot trainees with a phaser."

"It's for their own good, and I just zap them a little," he said, smiling big and fluttering his eyes. "Please?"

"Fine."

"How are things at the station?" His home, Charybdis Station, was going through some changes as it shifted from a mercenary base to an independent planet. Selene and the others were right in the middle of it all.

"Politics are boring," she said. "I've been working on training Hack's soldiers, and that's much more interesting."

Morgan snorted. "Of course you'd rather fight and train than sit through meetings." He pulled his long, blond hair into a bun at the top of his head. "Is Xu still enjoying school?"

Selene had recently adopted a young orphan. People had been surprised, but Morgan knew his girl. She was a good mom.

"He is. He's very smart and likes to read," she said. "He's also already better at defense training than the other children his age."

"Proud mama," he teased her. "You're doing great with him, Selene, which is no surprise really. You put up with me."

"He's part of my family," she said. "You are too, Morgan."

"I know," he said, smiling tenderly. "I'm the little brother that likes to annoy you. At least Shae worships the ground you walk on. You don't have to deal with pranks from him."

Shae was her biological brother and had recently moved in with her at Charybdis Station. He was a good person, just very young and sheltered.

"True," she said.

"How is he settling in?"

"He tried training with the fresh recruits. It... didn't go well. He isn't good at hurting others, even in training."

"Oh no," he said. "He had his heart set on being a soldier like you."

"Then he worked with medical to become an assistant. That also ended badly. Apparently, he doesn't take orders well."

Morgan winced, feeling sorry for the young Siren. "What did he try next?"

"Diplomacy," she said.

"Oh, fuck," Morgan said. The young man was way too sarcastic to be a diplomat.

"Correct. Now, he's working as Leti's assistant. He's actually very good at it."

"That's unexpected. I guess Leti can use all the help he can get."

"Morgan!" Dru came through his door without knocking. The captain of the Blue Sparrow carried her vexal newt, Monty, on her shoulder. "Are you seriously shooting at Quinn and Hazel every time one of their tells pops up? I overheard them talking in the commons."

"It's a common technique, Dru," Selene said from the vid-screen. Morgan grinned. His big sister was the best. "He has his phaser on the lowest setting, and it really is for their own good."

"Fine," Dru said, narrowing her eyes on Morgan. "I've got my eyes on you, Murray. I still remember when you first joined our crew on the Blue Solace. You put syrup on my pillow."

Morgan shot her a shocked look. "You think that was me? That was Lucas." His best friend had joined the crew at the same time as him.

"Bullshit, pretty boy. I'm watching you." She glared one more time, then spun and stomped out of his room.

"You were the one who put syrup on her pillow," Selene said.

"Your point? Lucas isn't here to defend himself."

The two chatted for a few more minutes and then ended the call. Morgan stared at the walls for a minute, then called Lucas.

"Hey, man," Lucas said. The Betonize-Cardinal hybrid looked good. He had lost an arm, an eye, and a leg on their last mission and was still recovering. Morgan didn't like to think how close he'd come to losing him.

"Have you married Draif yet?"

"The better question would be: have I even kissed

Draif yet," Lucas said with a self-deprecating look. "We're getting closer every day, but it's slow-going."

"You two will get there," Morgan said. "I spent a lot of time with him while you were being lazy. He has trust issues, and he's demisexual. Just be patient."

"Wow," Lucas said. "You were your normal insulting, asshole self right there *and* a mature adult. What's happening?"

Morgan stuck his tongue out at his friend. "I'm a kickass adult, man. Get it straight."

"Something's up with you," Lucas said. "I don't know what, but I'll figure it out."

"Oh, no," Morgan said. "I just got a message. Dru needs me."

"I'm looking right at you," Lucas said. "You're a fat-mouth liar."

Morgan leaned forward and *oops* the call ended.

He put his shoes on, then left his room, unable to deal with the quiet tonight. Usually, it didn't bother him, but lately, being alone had gotten downright lonely. Stupid Lucas and his comments.

He headed for the bridge.

Linc knelt on the floor, doing his own session of meditating. As the pilot, he stayed in or near the bridge, but he usually had more free time when they were in deep space. The young hybrid looked like a small bit of fluff. He had white, feline ears atop his head like a Cardinal, as well as the tail to match. A light, pale white fuzz covered his skin, showing his Grell heritage, and his large green eyes and little fangs were inherited from his Betonize hybrid father.

Morgan knew that, though the man looked cute and sweet, he had a mean right hook and very few tells.

"Hey, Morgan," Linc said, eyes popping open. "Do you think I should get a chicken like Dannol? It just doesn't seem right to fly a ship without a chicken."

Morgan blinked, shaking his head. He was also a sweetheart. "I think that only works for Dannol," Morgan said. Linc slumped, disappointed. "We'll grab you something at the next spaceport. Maybe a hamster." The young man perked back up. Damn it. When did his trainees' feelings start to matter?

"Remember, I'll be here two hours before breakfast for your hand-to-hand combat training," Morgan said, shaking his head.

"Yes, sir," Linc said with a grin. "It's rough, but I'm glad you don't shoot me anymore like you do Quinn and Hazel."

"Everyone's a critic," Morgan muttered, leaving the bridge. He quickly made his way to the commons. Quinn and Hazel smiled from the couch they were sprawled on. Lerais fiddled with some electronic device at a table in the corner, and Dru sat across from her husband, talking to someone on her comm.

Alois ate his meal at his own table, so Morgan warmed up his dinner and joined the Blue Sparrow's lieutenant.

"I miss Juniper," Alois said, sighing as he moved the nasty lumps of food around. "Remember his beef stew?"

"It actually had beef in it," Morgan said, spooning up a bite of unidentifiable meat. "How could I forget?"

"I can't get over how well the three newbies are doing," Alois said, watching Hazel and Quinn talk.

"It's because I'm awesome, but they still have work to do. Linc is good with hand-to-hand, but seriously needs work with the phaser. Hazel is getting better at defense, but she needs to keep working on both shooting and offence. Quinn has a lot of potential. She's definitely our fighter, but she still gives too much away. She is really good with a rifle though."

"Fuck me," Dru said, sitting. "You sound... responsible."

Alois gave him a look of horror. "Not our Morgan," he said, raising his fist in the air. "Please, by the gods, not our Morgan."

Morgan rolled his eyes. "Trust me. This wasn't my idea. Why did you and Hack have to go and give me authority? Don't you know how badly that could go?" He gave Dru a pointed look. "Well, Captain?"

Dru preened at being called captain, then she seemed to wilt. "I'm going to sound like my fucking mother here, but it can't be helped." She scowled at him. "You have too much damn potential to waste it. It's sure as shit easier to stay in your comfort zone, but you'll never grow that way. You're doing a good job, and Hack and I both know you're an asset, so get used to it."

"Wow," Alois said after a moment of silence. "Was that difficult to say, Dru?"

"Yes," she said simply. "I hate fucking pep talks. That's Hack's deal."

"You need to get out of *your* comfort zone, Captain," Morgan said. "Be the captain we all know you can be."

"You suck," Dru said, standing. She dropped a kiss to his forehead. "You're still a damn good weapons specialist though. You're going to have to deal with the anxiety and the upset tummy, pretty boy."

"It's an ulcer," Morgan said, affronted. "Probably from this shitty food."

"Sure," she said, walking away. "If that makes you feel better."

"She's ridiculous." He sniffed. Alois just laughed at him.

After somehow managing to eat the shitty dinner, Morgan went back to his quarters, ready for his new favorite bad habit. He braided his hair, then sprawled on his bed.

He pulled a picture up on his comm. Wyatt Morrick glowed with happiness, and his smile completely transformed his plain face. His brown hair blew in the wind, and his sweet brown eyes sparkled with good humor.

He hugged a medium-sized dog with long, shaggy grey fur. Its tongue hung out, and the dog looked as happy as her owner. According to Wyatt's mom, her name was Luna, and Wyatt had raised her from a puppy.

Morgan stared at the picture for a long time before setting his comm on his nightstand. He didn't feel so lonely with Wyatt Morrick's smiling face watching over him as he fell asleep.

$\mathcal{M}$ organ sat at the small conference table in Dru's office with the rest of the crew, anger churning in his gut. The CEO of the Galactic Association of Compassionate Professionals filled the vid-screen. Reginald Foster's face was lined with worry, and he looked older than his forty-two years.

"Ralen Jevio has worked with GACP for over ten years. I find it hard to believe he would just abandon Wyatt's medical team, but that's what our investigation determined," Foster said.

"Have you spoken with Jevio?" Dru asked.

"I did, and he claims he's innocent. He says the team only recently went missing and that he had begun the process of reporting it," Foster said.

"Do you believe him?" Alois looked doubtful.

"No," Foster said, looking frustrated. "I want to, but the investigation discovered they've been missing for almost two months now. None of our contacts on Tammol have answered our calls. Communications seem to be down. We sent a team, but they didn't make it far before turning around. Unknown ships fired on them, and they barely made it back. The whole planet has gone crazy."

"Isn't it always crazy?" Morgan asked, worried about Wyatt. The planet's history was a bloody one, and peaceful times were few and far between.

"It is to a degree, but the two groups at war understand why we're there. They treat our people with respect and are seldom a problem. We have no political agenda, only a will to treat the injured."

"What kind of information has Jevio given you?" Hazel asked, eyes calculating.

"He gave us the name of the village they were last at, but we don't think that's right. Wyatt's reports contradict all of Ralen's, and Wyatt is usually so meticulous. He always sends his reports to Ralen and my assistant, Gina. The problem is that we don't know where they were last because Wyatt's last report never got to us."

"It sounds like Ralen has something to hide," Hazel said. "He's lied about the timeline and likely about their last known location. Either he's extremely incompetent, or he's trying to keep you from finding them."

Foster slumped in his seat. "You're likely right. I've forwarded the information the investigators managed to gather. Ralen is on unpaid leave until we figure out what's happened. He has an apartment in Pagent's Distillery on Rueal."

"We'll go have a chat with him," Dru said.

Morgan smiled, and Alois kicked him. The Dedril mouthed, *"creepy smile."*

Morgan ignored him, pleased at the idea of getting his hands on Jevio. He didn't know exactly what the man had done, but his gut told him Jevio had something to do with Wyatt's disappearance.

"Thank you, Captain," Foster said. "If you need anything, please don't hesitate to ask. We're fond of Wyatt, and his whole team is full of wonderful people. I want them home safely."

"We'll do what we can," Dru said, then ended the call. "Okay, there is definitely something up with Ralen Jevio."

"Why would he want to get rid of a team of do-gooders?" Quinn spun in her chair, face reflecting her confusion. "What kind of motive would he have? Has anyone checked his financials? What about his specific relationship with Wyatt?"

"Good questions," Dru said.

"Wyatt's mother said he was dating someone, remember? She said he'd started a new post a while ago and he's been dating someone," Morgan said. He fought back a growl. Damn, that fact bothered the shit out of him. "Think about it. Who would he be able to spend time with? Who would he not want to tell his mother about?"

"Oh, fuck," Hazel said. "What do you want to bet he was dating Jevio, his supervisor? That's not something you would want to admit to mom unless it was super stable and serious."

"Hmm, Jevio looks high class too," Alois said, pulling his file up on the vid-screen. "He's mostly human and comes from a wealthy, powerful family on the planet Rueal. They dominate one of the four largest cities on the planet, Pagent's Distillery. They're in the... well... liquor business. Everyone in the city is, just look at the damn name."

"If his family has wealth, power, and influence, it could create a problem for us," Dru said, troubled. "What if they didn't want their mostly human son to date a hybrid? This could get dangerous."

"It's not like we're just going to walk in and ask our questions," Lerais pointed out. "We send in a buffet of young, pretty things. Get the man alone, then have that conversation you want. Plus, we can get backup if needed. Jody has some of her people stationed in Sugarworm System."

Morgan liked Lerais's sister Jody. She was a good woman and ran her own, much smaller, mercenary band. They tended to focus on rescue missions.

"I like that idea," Dru said. "Okay, get to work, guys. Brainstorm some ideas, and we'll meet again tonight. We have a little time to put together a plan. I'll send all the files to each of you as soon as Foster gets them to me."

Everyone stood, heading for the door.

"Morgan, I need you for a minute," Dru said.

Morgan sat back down and watched the others leave. Once the door closed behind them, he faced Dru. "What?"

"What?" She mocked him. "What is with you and Wyatt Morrick?"

"Nothing. I've never met the guy."

"You seem to take this awfully personal, and I saw his picture on your comm when I caught you taking a break in the commons."

Morgan groaned. How embarrassing. "Okay, so I might have a teeny tiny crush on the guy."

Dru pressed her lips together, staring at him. Monty sat atop her head, watching him steadily. "You have a crush?"

"Come on," he said. "The man's smart, kind, and handsome. What's not to like? Did you see his cute, pointy little ears?"

Dru couldn't hold her laughter in any longer. "Oh, fuck. This is golden. Pretty boy Morgan has a crush on the plain, do-gooder doctor."

"He's not plain," Morgan protested. "Not when he smiles. It lights up his whole damn face."

She laughed harder but eventually managed to compose herself. "Okay, so you have a crush. Try to keep it steady, Murray. I'll keep you on point, so you can have your fun with Jevio. Despite Foster's hesitancy, I think we all know good old Ralen had something to do with Wyatt's team disappearing."

"Oh yeah. You know, Wyatt's mom talked to Jevio when Wyatt first disappeared. He told her that she was overreacting and suffocating her son. Can you believe the man's gall?"

"Seriously. There is something suspicious about him."

18

"Yeah?" Morgan grumbled, standing and heading for the door.

"Morgan," she said.

He turned. "What?"

She smiled sadly. "Are you going to be okay when we go to the planet? Tammol? Its current state is a lot like Union Station was when you were a kid."

"We've been to a ton of war-ravaged planets. Why would it bother me now?"

"You've been different lately. More thoughtful than usual," she said.

"I'll be fine, Dru," Morgan said, leaving.

Alois leaned against the wall next to the door. "I hear someone has a crush."

"Eavesdropping, Lieutenant?"

"It's the only way to hear the best gossip," Alois said, falling into place beside him as Morgan headed for the training room. "You don't have to tell me—I'm just being nosy—but what happened when you were a kid?"

"My parents died in the Gang Wars on Union Station."

Alois stopped him and pulled him into a hug. Morgan froze, but the Dedril just squeezed him once and let him go. "Okay. I can understand Dru's concern now. Tammol is going through a very similar situation. I can see it bringing up bad memories."

"Why are we having *feeling* conversations? I wasn't thinking about it at all until she brought it up, but now I *am* thinking about it. Damn nosy people."

His parents hadn't made it off Union Station, but

he'd make sure Wyatt stayed alive. Assuming he wasn't already dead. His chest hurt at that thought.

"We'll save him, Morgan. That's what we're here for, and honestly, I think everyone's afraid of what will happen if we go home without him. Leti will string us up for sure."

3

SUGARWORM SYSTEM, PLANET TAMMOL

yatt Morrick clutched Luna tight with one arm, burying his face in her dirty, grey fur. The little girl curled against his side pressed against him, shaking with fear. He pulled her as close as possible, offering what comfort he could.

Estella was alone now, her family dead and her home destroyed.

Every person in the cave system huddled down, staying as small and quiet as possible. The troop of soldiers walked past the hidden entrance, loud and obnoxious. Fear etched furrows into the faces of the injured Tammolians and their families.

The surviving members of his team hid it better. Maybe they were just numb to it now.

Kiki crouched beside him, face blank and empty. He remembered when his best friend and guard laughed and joked. Her curly red hair would bounce as a flush spread across her pale skin. Joe'd had a way of making the too serious woman smile and blush.

He missed that woman so much, but didn't know how to bring her back. Not without Joe.

The rest of his team focused on keeping the Tammolians secured and silent. A million heartbeats later, the troop passed.

Kiki moved silently to the mouth of the cave and poked her head through the foliage. She turned and nodded, then inched outside to continue her watch.

Everyone breathed a sigh of relief.

Wyatt let go of Luna and sanitized his hands again. His dog gave him a soft woof, then went to stand guard with Kiki. Estella settled back against the wall, brown eyes focused on him as he moved back to one of his critical patients.

Rasha had taken multiple shots to her chest and stomach when the village was attacked. Usually, they would have been able to stabilize her and fix her up quickly, but they were normally in a medical room. The cave didn't offer much sanitation, supplies, or technology. They only had what they had managed to carry with them when they ran.

He spread more micro-healer across the wound, wishing again they had the more potent stuff. Rasha smiled at him despite her pain and weariness. Her husband, Dashel, held her hand, their two small children huddled against him. Wyatt didn't have the heart to tell them that without more supplies, they would lose her. She had maybe two weeks left.

"Did you get something to eat, Wyatt?"

Jane was one of his nurses and a good friend. Her left arm was broken. He had straightened it and put it in a makeshift cast, but the woman wouldn't stop. She stayed at his side and continued helping as much as she could. He wished he could spare her the pain medicine she needed.

"Wyatt," she said again, cupping his little round belly. "Did you eat? I know you want to conserve food, but you need to think about this little peanut too."

"He did not," Rasha said roughly. "Think of your baby, doctor."

"I'll sit with her," Jane said, eyes sympathetic. "Go get a meal from Pela."

"Fine," Wyatt said, grumbling. "Come on, Estella. Let's go eat."

They slowly weaved through the pallets, and he stopped to check on a patient here and there. No one else was as badly off as Rasha, but they needed more supplies if they wanted to live longer than a few months. The situation was getting worse.

He reached Pela, another nurse, and smiled at the woman. Where Kiki was empty and numb, Pela was full of fear since the attack. She had always been so confident and bold. She jumped when he tapped her on the shoulder.

"Pela," he said gently. "Are you okay?"

"Those were the same soldiers," she said, voice shaky. "They're the ones that killed Lolani, Ron, and Joe. That... *thing* was probably with them."

When the village had been attacked by off-world soldiers, the second medical team were the first to die. They had been working with a patient when the attack happened, a young man who had stepped on a mine.

He'd lost his leg, but Lolani was sure they could save him. Wyatt had left her to it and went to care for their other patients.

Then came the attack.

Lolani had been a magnificent doctor. She'd been young, but so damn talented and kind. Ron was the second team's guard, and the man had had a thing for Lolani. Watching them flirt back and forth had made his heart warm.

Joe and Pela were her nurses. Pela managed to run, but Joe hadn't even tried. Kiki's husband had died trying to protect their patient.

"They've gone, Pela," he said, dragging his attention to the present. He found himself having to do that more and more each day that passed. "We're okay for now."

She nodded, still shaking. "I hate being so afraid." She took a deep breath. "You two need food, right? I'll get you an MRE, Dr. Wyatt." She turned to their supplies and quickly dug one out. She handed it to him, along with a fork. She got a smaller, child-sized MRE and handed it to Estella, giving the girl a shaky smile before turning back to him. "I'm about to make the rounds for dinner, doctor."

"Thank you, Pela," he said. He reached for her hand, steadying it in his own. "We'll make it out of this. When GACP finds out what Ralen did, they'll punish him. I swear to you that I'll make sure he will pay."

The woman gave him a half-hearted smile and gathered up the day's dinner rations. Wyatt found a clear spot for Estella and himself, then scarfed down his meal. It tasted like crap, but his belly said it was oh, so good. His second nurse, Rune, sat next to him with his own meal.

The large hybrid was still favoring his left leg, and Wyatt pushed away his guilt. If he had been faster, his friend wouldn't have gotten injured protecting him. Rune grabbed Wyatt's empty container and scooped half of his own food onto it.

"Rune, no," Wyatt said. "I've eaten my portion."

"Gotta think of the baby, Doc," he said with a sweet smile. He handed it to Wyatt. "Eat up."

His gnawing stomach told him to get to it, but Rune was a big guy. He needed his fuel.

"Rune," Wyatt said again.

"Deal with it, Doc," Rune responded. "It goes in your belly, or it goes on the ground."

Estella patted Wyatt's belly and gave him a no-nonsense look. Rune chuckled and Wyatt gave in.

Wyatt glared at the smiling giant the entire second it took him to polish off the food. "Happy?"

"Fucking ecstatic," Rune said with a smirk, pointed ear tips twitching.

"Rune, how can you all not hate me?" Wyatt asked. "Even Kiki doesn't hate me."

Estella leaned against him, eating her own meal slowly.

"First, you and Kiki have been best friends for a long time, and I've been your friend for years. We could never hate you. Second, it's not your fault, Doc. Jevio chose to abandon us here. He even fucking *told* you why he was doing it. Hell, we all know he has something to do with those off-world soldiers too, maybe even that creature they have with them." The big man shrugged. "You know Mr. Foster would have sent people for us by now if he knew. It's all on that dickhead."

"I'm the one who got pregnant," Wyatt said.

He had been so flattered when Ralen started paying him attention. Wyatt knew he wasn't the most attractive person. He wasn't ugly, he was just… ordinary. Ralen had said all the right things. Then Wyatt got pregnant.

"It takes two for that, right? Maybe three, depending on how kinky you are." Rune nudged him with his shoulder. "You being pregnant isn't the problem anyway. Dickhead chose to basically murder a whole medical team just to avoid his responsibilities. That's on him. We all get it."

Wyatt leaned over and kissed the big man's cheek. "I love you, Rune. You're the best."

Rune grinned. "We have your back, Doc. Try not to worry too much."

When Estella finished her meal, Wyatt left Rune to his half meal and did his rounds, the little Tammolian at his side.

He made sure to smile and laugh as much as he could. He made silly faces and told jokes to get some smiles from the kids. He held his patients' hands as they told him of their lives and the family that wasn't with them—those that stayed behind and were likely dead.

His team had managed to bring most of their

patients with them with the help of the patients' families, but some of the able-bodied had stayed behind to distract the attacking soldiers.

Wyatt had worked with the GACP for a while now and had never been in this kind of situation. He had never lost a team member before, let alone three. Tammol wasn't peaceful by any means. The Commonwealth technically controlled the planet at the moment, but it was in a constant state of civil unrest and had been for the past twenty years. The Resistance fought the Commonwealth at every turn, and the planet's population suffered for it.

Despite the constant bloodshed, the two sides both benefitted from the GACP's presence, so they treated them well.

These new attackers, though, were *not* Tammolians. They quite noticeably didn't have the thick, leathery, brown skin, and small horns of the planet's natives. The attackers were all human, trained in combat, and merciless. They were someone's soldiers.

Jane grabbed Wyatt's arm as he walked past her and Rasha. "Sit down for a second, Wyatt. Rest your feet."

He reluctantly sat, noticing Estella was about to drop. The eight-year-old was determined to stay at his side, but she was still a little girl. Rasha was sleeping, and her family did their best to follow suit. The youngest sucked his thumb, sleepy eyes locked on Wyatt.

"What do you think Garen's eating back home," Wyatt asked. Jane's husband loved his food and worked in a fancy restaurant on Rueal. He also loved his wife

27

and had to be going crazy. Before the attack, the two had talked on the comm or vid-screen every single night.

"That jerk is probably eating a big bowl of dumplings. He knows how much I love them," she said. "I know he must have contacted Gina or Mr. Foster by now. They'll send help, Wyatt. I know it." She watched him for a minute. "What are you going to do when they come?"

"Help move our patients to a better facility."

"I mean about the baby."

"I don't know. I'm four months along. I guess I'll keep getting bigger until this thing pops out."

"Is that your professional jargon, Dr. Morrick?"

Wyatt made a face. "Dr. Morrick is my dad. You know you're supposed to call me Dr. Wyatt."

"I guess your mom and dad have contacted the GACP too, huh?" Jane settled her head on Wyatt's shoulder.

"I know Mom will have. My dad barely knows I exist. He won't know I'm in trouble or care enough to do anything about it."

"You never talk about him," Jane said, eyes full of sympathy.

Wyatt shrugged. "Nothing to say. He's a brilliant scientist who cares more about his work than his family."

"That doesn't sound like nothing."

Wyatt swallowed his tears. He was so tired, so scared. "It's nothing, Jane. Absolutely nothing."

She leaned up and kissed his forehead. A wet dog

tongue joined in.

"Eww, Luna," Jane said. "Wait your turn."

Wyatt laughed and hugged his dog. She had been with him through thick and thin for the past three years. He didn't know what he'd do without her. He looked around the cave again. "I need to finish my rounds. Get some sleep, crazy lady."

"Will do," she said, lying down on the hard ground near Rasha. "You do the same."

"Estella, stay here and sleep," he said. The little girl ignored him, getting back to her feet, hand in Luna's fur for balance. She shook her head, chin pointed up.

Wyatt sighed and went back to work, followed by his shadow. They had been in this cave system for two months. Something had to give if they were to survive much longer. He finished checking on his last patient and noticed Rune relieving Kiki from her watch. The tall woman settled in a corner to sleep. He sat beside her, promptly getting a lapful of Luna. The dog needed her rest too.

"Kiki," he whispered. "We have to do something. Our supplies are running out, and we have no way to call for help. I don't think anyone's coming."

"I know," she said softly. "I'll start scouting further out. If I can find a workable communicator, I can contact Foster."

"You can't go alone, and Luna isn't much protection," he said. He kissed his girl's head, hoping she wasn't offended. "I can come with you."

"No." Kiki's voice left no room for negotiation.

"Pela is too jumpy, Jane has a broken arm, and Rune is still limping."

"I'll go alone, and Rune will stand guard here," she said. "I'm your security, Wyatt. I'm the one who protects the team. It's my call."

"I don't want to lose you, Kiki," he said in a small voice. He lay down beside Kiki and curled around her, pulling Estella down with him. Luna curled against his back as usual.

"You worry too much, Wy," she said, wrapping her arms around him and the little girl. "Believe it or not, I can take care of myself. I'll find a comm or supplies. How long does Rasha have?"

"Two weeks at the most," he whispered.

"I'll start tomorrow."

yatt made sure Kiki ate before she left for the day, Luna following behind her. He kissed his dog and his friend. "Make sure you two stay safe. We need help, but we need you both too."

Luna tilted her head, tongue lolling, and Kiki sighed. "We'll be careful. Fuck, you're worse than my mother."

"There's my little girl," he said, pinching her cheeks. "Love you."

Her mouth tilted up a bit. "Love you too." She grabbed her bag, and the two slipped out of the cave. Rune stood right at the entrance, keeping an eye out for soldiers. Wyatt watched them go until they disappeared into the woods.

"Have some faith, Doc," Rune said.

"How can I after everything that's happened?" Wyatt tilted his face up toward the sun. Living in a cave had a lot of downsides.

The large man shook his head. "That's when you need faith the most."

"Okay. I'll work on that," Wyatt said sarcastically, making Rune laugh. "What will you do when you get home, Rune?"

Most of his team lived temporarily on Rueal since it was the closest to Tammol. It made leaving on their off weeks a lot easier. Wyatt, Kiki, Joe, and Rune always got together to watch movies and eat at the local cafés and restaurants. It wouldn't be the same without Joe.

"First thing I'll do is take a shower," Rune said with a smile. "Then eat a ton of food." He turned Wyatt around and pushed him back toward the cave. "Get in there where's it's safe, Doc. I've got this."

"Fine," Wyatt said, pouting.

Before he entered the cave, a rat carcass just outside the entrance caught his eye. He bent to look at it, noting the emaciated body. It was a dried husk, empty of all fluids. It hadn't been there two days ago when he'd snuck out to talk to Kiki.

He shook his head, body shaking at the knowledge of how close they'd come to dying yesterday. Those troops really had been the ones that had attacked the village. The creature had been with them.

Wyatt had seen people shot, stabbed, blown up, drowned, and set on fire. He'd thought he'd seen it all. When the attack happened, there were plenty of shots fired and grenades thrown, but that wasn't what haunted him. He looked back at Rune, catching his attention, and nudged the rat. The large man paled.

"Fuck," he said. "It was them yesterday."

"I had hoped Pela was wrong."

"What is that thing, Doc?" It wasn't the first time they had asked that question. "It sure as shit looked human, except for those weird eyes. It was dressed just like the others too. They're part of some kind of military unit."

"I don't know, Rune," Wyatt answered quietly. "I've never seen anything like it. Based on appearance, it was a human male, but no human could have survived being shot and stabbed."

The villagers had fought back with a vengeance to protect their homes and families. He'd seen Kiki shoot the creature in the fucking head, and it just shrugged it off.

"I've never seen any species or hybrid do what it did," Wyatt said.

Rune shivered. "It reminds me of creepy vampire stories from Old-Earth. It drew all the blood and fluids from people right into it. Didn't have to touch them either. Just *called* it to him, like a stray dog. Fuck. That shit is messed up."

"Agreed," Wyatt said.

"Get back in the cave, Doc," Rune said. "It's safer there."

Wyatt didn't argue this time. That rat was reason enough to hide for the rest of his life. Estella waited on him at the entrance, and Jane and Pela walked around the cavern, checking on patients.

"Ready to get to work?" he asked the girl. She nodded and they got to it.

Infection had set into the wound of an older man.

33

Wyatt used a bit more of their precious micro-healer. He hoped Kiki found something. Rasha's pain was worse today, and Wyatt was out of the stronger meds. He gave her the mild ones and held her hand through the worst of it. Eventually, she settled into sleep.

Dashel looked defeated. "She's not going to make it, is she?"

"I won't lie," Wyatt said, nodding to Estella. She pulled Rasha's two kids away, settling them in a corner. "If we don't get more supplies, she won't make it. That being said, Kiki is out looking for something now, so don't give up hope. Your wife is a fighter. She'll hang on as long as she can, and you need to encourage her."

"I will," he said. "I can't do this without her. I won't let her go without a fight."

"Me neither," Wyatt said, squeezing the man's hand.

Later that night, Kiki came back with a small bag of medical supplies and a sack of torgon fruit. The thick-skinned fruit wasn't the tastiest thing growing on Tammol, but it was a welcome treat.

The medical bag had some potent anti-bacterial healer that he instantly applied to the worst of Rasha's wounds. She slept on, but she didn't look quite so pale.

Most importantly, he noticed the hope in her husband's eyes and the smiles on the faces of the Tammolians. Rasha was a good woman and their friend.

After his rounds, he grabbed dinner and went outside the cave to talk to Kiki. The tall woman perched amidst large ferns, eyes constantly surveying the surrounding area. Luna lay at her side, completely hidden by the large, purple leaves of the plant. Wyatt knelt next to them.

"Thank you, Kiki," he said. "Rasha stands a better chance now, and the others have a bit more hope."

"They shouldn't," she said, voice rough and frightened.

Wyatt's mouth dropped open in shock. "What?"

"That creature and its soldiers are killing off every Tammolian they come across," she said. "I found two villages today. Every person was dead and the villages were ransacked. None of the comms work. There's no communication."

"What does it want? Do you think the Resistance or the Commonwealth hired the creature and the soldiers?"

"No," she said with certainty. "These men kill without discrimination. Every living person dies, then they take food, medical supplies, and the livestock." Her eyes filled with sadness. "They're all just empty husks or rotting corpses. All those lives gone now, and what can we do about it? Nothing. Nothing will kill that bastard."

Wyatt was quiet a moment, debating. "I've been working on something," he said, reluctantly. "Did I ever tell you my dad works with viruses? He researches them and creates cures and vaccinations."

"No," she said, watching him curiously. "You never talk about him, just your mom. Working with viruses is kind of awesome."

"Yeah. He's great," Wyatt said flatly. He knew his dad did good work, but his heart still had trouble understanding why Wyatt wasn't important enough for a fucking call or visit. "The point is, when I was in school, my dumb ass took a lot of classes on virology."

"To feel closer to him?"

"Probably," he said. "I definitely didn't major in psychology. Anyway, I have an idea. There's an old virus that we studied. It was used as chemical warfare, but it's long gone now. We studied the structure of it, and it primarily affected humans. It was nasty. It would basically cause the infected person's blood to boil. All it took was ninety seconds, and the person would die horrifically."

"What's your idea?"

"I can create a poison," Wyatt said. "With the right ingredients."

"What are you saying?"

"The creature seemed to consume all the blood of its victims. It just soaked into the thing's body. I think I can kill it by affecting its blood. The virus happens so fast and at the cellular level. I don't think it could regenerate."

"Assuming it works, how would we keep the virus from spreading?"

"It wouldn't be the virus, just inspired from it."

"What do you need?"

"I've made you a list," he said. "A lot of the ingredients can be found in any common med bay, but there are a few that will be harder to find. I don't know if the villages in the area will have it all, but they'll have some. I've been studying the local fauna while I've been here, so I can find some substitutes for the rarer ingredients."

"If we need to, I can travel to one of the cities. It'll take a couple of days and it's riskier, but it might be our only hope."

"I'm surprised the Commonwealth haven't tried to deal with this creature themselves. They should have their own soldiers pouring through the area."

"That's why I want to see the closest city. We spend most of our time in the cave. A million things could be happening and we wouldn't know it. I have a feeling those off-world soldiers are just doing clean-up now. Tammol is a small planet with mostly rural villages. If they were going to take it over, they would start with the cities, right?"

"I don't know, Kiki," he said, horror filling him. "I don't think I *want* to know."

5

SUGARWORM SYSTEM, PLANET RUEAL

*M*organ walked through the streets of Pagent's Distillery. The city was posh for sure. Fancy boutiques and restaurants dominated the shopping district, but there were still a few unsavory venues.

Morgan, Quinn, and Alois, dressed in their best, were outside one, watching the customers come and go. The Barley Button was a small, exclusive brothel disguised as a bar.

Currently, the bouncer was throwing a young Wello man out the door. "I know that fucker is in there," the man yelled. "Let me see him. My wife's missing, and that bastard knows something."

"Mr. Jevio doesn't want to talk to you," the bouncer said, a growl in his voice. "I suggest you leave before we call the police."

Morgan and Alois exchanged a glance, and Morgan hurried forward. He grabbed the man's raised arm, stopping the punch aimed for the bouncer.

"My friend's drunk, sir," he said. "I'll make sure he gets home and calms down. I'm so sorry for the inconvenience."

"Who the hell are you?" The man struggled in his grasp.

Morgan bent forward. "A friend. Now shut up. We'll never get to Jevio with you causing a scene."

The man went slack instantly. "I'm so sorry," he said to the bouncer. "I've had so much to drink tonight."

The bouncer sneered and turned his back on them. Morgan pulled the man to where Alois and Quinn waited in the alley. "Who are you?" Morgan asked.

"My name is Garen."

"Who's your wife?" Alois asked.

"Her name is Jane. She works for the GACP."

"Does she work with Wyatt Morrick?" Quinn asked.

"Yeah. He's the lead doctor in her medical team."

"You're trying to figure out where they are?" Morgan said, nodding.

"Yes. Ralen Jevio knows something. He dismisses me every time I call or message him, but he has to know something. There's no way my Jane wouldn't talk to me for two months. We talk every night."

"Listen," Alois said. "We're searching for Morrick, so we're on it. Go home, and we'll let you know when we find them, alright?"

Garen stared at him in amazement. "Are you really that stupid? I'm not going home until I know she's safe."

Morgan chuckled, and Alois glared at him before

turning back to Garen. "This isn't going to be pretty. You sure you want in?"

"Yes," he said, rolling his eyes. "What's your plan? I assume you're going to talk to Jevio, right?"

"We are," Morgan said. "We were about to go in and lure him out."

Garen looked the three of them up and down. "Send her," he said, nodding to Quinn. "Jevio likes men and women, but I heard a waitress say he was all over the girls tonight. She's beautiful. He'll make a move on her in a heartbeat. The brothel girls are pretty, but not that pretty."

Quinn did look good tonight. The Fallon-Silet hybrid's golden hair cascaded around her bare shoulders. Gold hoops decorated her pointed ears, and her golden skin sparkled like it was covered in glitter. Her black dress was skimpy, covering just what it had to. The woman looked vapid and easily persuaded.

"Don't hurt him until he's out here, Quinn," Morgan said, grinning at the woman's disgusted look. "Flutter your lashes and channel your sexiness." Morgan made a little moue and fluttered his eyes.

Alois clapped. "Aww. Who's a cute boy? Who's a cute boy?"

Quinn laughed. "You two are idiots, but don't worry, Garen. I've got this." She shook her head and walked toward Barley Buttons, hips swaying.

Fifteen minutes later, she walked back out on the arm of Ralen Jevio. She giggled, clutching his arm.

"You are so smart," she said in a breathy voice. As

they passed the alley, she stumbled. "Oh no." She pouted. "My shoe."

When he looked down to see what was wrong, she shoved him into the alley.

"What the fuck?" Jevio said.

Morgan covered his mouth and dragged him farther into the alley. At the very back, he released the man and pushed him hard against the brick wall.

"Hi there, Mr. Jevio," he said jovially. "I hope you're having a good evening."

"What's the meaning of this?" His eyes found Garen, and he glared at the man. "I've already told you. Your wife just doesn't want to talk to you. I can't help it if your marriage sucks."

Quinn kneed him in the groin.

Morgan winced in reluctant sympathy as the man doubled over, moaning. "Ouch," Morgan said. "Did that hurt?"

"Where is Morrick and his team?" Alois wore his serious lieutenant face.

"What are you talking about?" Jevio asked, voice wheezing with pain. "Talk to the GACP." Morgan punched him in the side. The man yelped, falling back against the wall.

"We did," Alois said. "They hired us to find the missing team. The team you lost."

"Why would they do that? I've told them everything I know," he said quickly, watching Quinn and Morgan. Garen kicked him in the knee, and Jevio fell into the mud, yelling.

"Charybdis soldiers aren't afraid to get our hands dirty," Alois said, smile menacing.

"Charybdis?" Fear crawled across Jevio's face. "Fuck, fuck, fuck."

"What's wrong, Mr. Jevio?" Morgan asked, squatting in front of the fallen man. Charybdis Station had a reputation, but this was a bit much.

"Listen, I didn't know anything about the Concords attacking when I sent them down there, okay? My uncle was the one who told them about Tammol. All I did was refuse to send the shuttle to pick them up when they needed to leave. Then I didn't notify Foster when the village was attacked. That's all, okay? The rest is on the Concords. I don't work for them. I swear."

Ice shot through Morgan's chest, but he kept the grin on his face. He patted Jevio's cheek. "See, you don't get hurt when you say something important. Now, let's start at the beginning. What did your uncle tell the Concords about Tammol?"

"The planet was ripe for the taking. I've worked with them through the GACP for a while and told my uncle all about them. The planet has been at war for over twenty years. They have no large space presence and only a few large cities. My uncle is friends with Admiral Sharp. He told him about Tammol. I didn't know anything about it."

"What do the Concords want with the planet?" Quinn nudged Jevio with her foot.

"They need a base. My uncle says they're spreading out and are going to start purifying the galaxy."

"That doesn't sound ominous at all," Garen said.

"Okay," Alois said, nodding. "Now tell us about the team. What exactly happened?"

"Listen," Jevio said. "They're probably dead by now. It doesn't really matter."

Quinn's foot shot out to kick his balls again, and Morgan punched him in the jaw.

"Oopsie," Quinn said. "I thought it was my turn."

Morgan shrugged. "I lost count of whose turn it is. Alois?"

"It was hers, Morgan. You'll have to skip your turn. Garen, you can hit him next, okay?"

"Thank you," Garen said politely.

It took a few minutes for Jevio to recover enough to talk. "Let's try that again," Alois said. "Tell us about the team. Tell us everything, even about your relationship with Morrick."

Jevio looked shocked. "How did you know about that?" He shook his head, scowling. "The little prick wasn't even a good lay. He's too damn shy to do anything right."

Morgan growled and grabbed Jevio's throat. "I suggest you stay on topic," he said, voice low.

"Yes, sir," Jevio squeaked. Morgan loosened his grip. "Wyatt got pregnant, and he wouldn't get rid of it. My parents would disown me if they knew I mixed our pure blood with a hybrid. I couldn't risk them finding out. The GACP pays shit. I can't lose my trust fund."

"Fucker," Quinn said, cheeks red with anger.

Morgan barely heard her. Wyatt was pregnant and stuck on a planet that was under attack. Worry churned in his stomach, and he mentally cursed

43

C.W. GRAY

himself. This was why he didn't want to fucking care about people.

"Don't judge me," Jevio said, cupping his crotch while cowering back from the angry woman. "I couldn't let him have the baby. Things started to get dicey on the planet. A neighboring village was attacked, but when the team called for an evacuation, I told him no. I told him I was going to report them all as dead. I destroyed the most recent reports and cut their lines of communication. Then I just let things happen. The Concords had already started their attack on the planet. He's long dead by now, okay? It's done."

"It's not done until we find them," Garen said. "Wyatt is a good man, and you used him. We'll find them, and you will pay."

"Anything else you want to share, Mr. Jevio?" Morgan asked pleasantly.

"The last village they were at is called Jarth. I lied to the GACP."

"Let's bring him in," Alois said, lifting the man.

"Bring him where?" Garen looked thunderous. "His family owns this city. Nothing will happen to him."

"We're bringing him to the GACP," Morgan said. "They'll know what to do with him. They're based on the other side of the planet, so his family will have less sway."

He patted the man on the back and pulled him away from the others. Alois and Quinn pulled Jevio to the alley entrance.

Morgan looked at Garen. "One way or another,

44

Jevio won't live long. Either the GACP deals with him or we will. Now, are you coming to Tammol with us?"

"Of course," he said. "I'm a cook, so I'm not the best fighter, but I can fire a phaser."

"A cook?" Morgan felt some small amount of hope. "That is perfect."

6

SUGARWORM SYSTEM, EN ROUTE TO
PLANET TAMMOL

"The GACP has started processing Jevio," Dru said. "By the time we get back from Tammol, they'll have finished a trial and sentenced him."

"Shouldn't they wait until we know if anyone on the team has been injured or died?" Hazel frowned. "What if they're all dead, and he's just charged with attempted murder?"

"They're not dead," Garen and Morgan said at the same time.

The rest of the crew gave them sympathetic looks. Morgan cleared his throat. "We should call in backup," Morgan said. "If the Concords have been down there for over two months now, there's no telling what we'll run into."

"We'll send Jody our destination," Dru said. "Let's not drag the Foxtail Mercenaries into this unless we have too. I know she's been reluctant to get involved in our war with the Concords."

"It's not that she doesn't want to, love," Lerais said. He looked pained.

"I know, baby," Dru said, smiling gently. "She has more than just herself to think about."

"We'll reach Tammol tonight. It's not far from Rueal," Linc said. "I'll do some preliminary scans before we land at Jarth."

"Good idea," Dru said. "I'll call Jody now. Put away the extra supplies we picked up and get some rest guys. I have a feeling things are about to get crazy. Alois, Morgan, and Lerais, please stay for the call. The rest of you guys can scram. Oh yeah. Garen, welcome aboard. We really appreciate your skills."

Garen laughed. "I've never been so well-received. I'll get to work on lunch."

The rest of the crew filed out, and Dru patched the call through to Jody. Lerais's sister was flat out awesome. The woman was big and beautiful and had the warmest heart of any mercenary in the galaxy. Her mercenaries solely focused on rescue jobs, especially those involving children.

Jody's smile filled the screen. "Hey, baby brother," she said. "It's nice to see you too, Dru. You all need help?"

"You know us so well," Dru said with a smile. "We're about to go into a precarious situation. You're the closest ally to us, so we wanted to ask you to be our touchstone."

"Of course," Jody said. "Where you going?"

"Tammol," Lerais said.

"That place isn't usually too bad," Jody said.

"The Concords are in the process of conquering it," Alois said. "They plan to use it as a base as they *purify* the galaxy."

"What. The. *Fuck*."

"That's what our source says," Dru said. "We'll be getting a firsthand view of it tonight. We're landing near a village named Jarth. If you don't mind, we'll touch base daily. Hopefully, we'll be in and out, but if the Concords have set up any air defense around the planet, it could get complicated."

"You miss a day and my ass is coming to get you personally," Jody said. "This is really bad, guys. The Concords have always been snotty little asswipes, but you're talking about some serious shit here."

"We don't know what's going on with them, Jody," Dru said. "There's something not right, and Charybdis Station is working on figuring it out. Until then, we do the best we can. I've updated General Hackett, but we appreciate your help. Hopefully, things go smoothly."

"Good luck," Jody said. Her face was troubled. "Love you, Lerais."

"Love you too, big sis," he said. "I'll stay on the comm with you as we land, alright?"

"Perfect." The call ended.

"We have extra supplies, the ship is in good condition, and we know our situation," Dru said. "Why do I feel like there's a shitstorm waiting on us?"

"Because there probably *is* a shitstorm waiting on us," Morgan said, gut churning. "We don't have a choice though. He's down there."

"We'll find your future husband, pretty boy. Don't worry." Dru smirked, worry melting away.

"THAT LANDING WASN'T MY BEST," Linc said, breathless.

Morgan stood, rolling his shoulders. "To be fair, our systems didn't detect their planetary defenses."

"Report," Dru ordered.

"No serious injuries to the crew," Alois said after a moment.

"Serious injuries to the ship," Lerais said, voice grim. "Our shields only took part of the damage. We're stuck on the ground until I can get this shit fixed. I'll let you know how long as soon as I can. Lost contact with Jody too, so she's probably on her way."

"I'm so sorry, Captain," Linc said, on the verge of tears.

Dru rolled her eyes. "For fuck's sake, Linc, we were shot to shit. There was only so much you could do, and you did it. We landed without casualties."

"Thank you, Captain," he said, blushing. The guy was just too cute.

"Where are we?"

"Right next to Jarth," Linc said. "Our scans showed a lot of movement north and west of here. The map shows that's where the two largest cities on the planet are. It's pretty dead right here."

"Were we spotted?"

"Probably. Their air defenses report encounters. They can likely track our trajectory."

"We need to get the ship out of here," Dru said. "Lerais, can she move at all?"

"Like a fucking shuttle," he said, disgusted. "We can fly her away from here, but she's not making it back into space anytime soon."

"Let me and Quinn out here," Morgan said. "We'll start tracking Wyatt."

"How far will the comms work, Lerais?"

"Planet-side only. The ship's communication system may connect to another ship as long as it's right outside the planet's atmosphere."

"Okay. Take a shuttle and your comms," Dru said. "We'll head south since our scans didn't show much movement there. We'll let you know when we find a good spot to hole up."

"Captain," Garen said. "I need to go too. Please."

Dru nodded. "Follow Morgan's instructions and let Quinn and him do the fighting."

"Yes, sir."

Morgan gathered his weapons and loaded the shuttle with food and medical supplies in case they found the medical team right away. Garen and Quinn joined him, and they unloaded from the ship, speeding into the village as the Blue Sparrow flew south. The village was empty, only corpses and broken buildings left. A hard rain fell through the trees, and the morning sun barely peeked through the clouds.

Garen and Morgan both jumped out and began checking bodies, looking for the medical team. Morgan was soaked in moments, but he took the time to check each corpse. These poor people had been dead for at least two months. He came across a strange corpse. The man looked like he had been mummified. His corpse was emaciated and empty of all fluids. He had never seen anything like it. He took pictures and moved on, searching for Wyatt.

"Morgan," Garen yelled. "I've found some of the medical team."

Morgan ran to him, stopping to stare at the four bodies in front of them. They resembled the strange one he had seen outside. There were three men and one woman. None of them were Wyatt.

He let out a sigh of relief, then saw Garen's tears. "Fuck. Is that Jane?"

"No," Garen said, wiping at his cheeks. "It's Dr. Lolani, her security guard Ron, and one of her nurses, Joe. I don't know who the fourth body is."

"Maybe a patient," Morgan said, eyes taking in the position of the bodies. Joe lay atop the patient, likely trying to protect him. Ron had fallen in front of the doctor, a phaser next to his dried hand. What the hell had happened to them?

"Come on," he said, finally. "Let's keep searching." They hunted for over an hour, but the village was empty of anything living. "Where would they have gone?"

"What if they were captured?" Quinn asked.

"It doesn't look like the Concords were taking prisoners," he said.

"Jane always said the villagers had little hidey holes they would go to when the fighting got bad. Any survivors would have gone there," Garen said.

"Let's branch out," Morgan said. "We can hide the shuttle and each take a direction. We'll avoid south for now. We'll be heading there soon enough anyway. It would likely be within a few miles of the village. I'll take north. Check in every fifteen minutes."

They split up, and Morgan headed through the thick forest, looking for signs of travel. It was clear several large groups had marched this way recently. MRE wrappers and other litter were thrown carelessly into the bushes. These were the Concords most likely. The survivors would be taking more care to hide themselves.

He bent down to pick up an empty casing and noticed a grey and white paw beneath a bush. He smiled wide, standing. "Luna?"

The dog poked her head out of the bushes, giving him a weary look. The poor thing was wet and dirty, rain pelting her. He knelt. "Hey, sweetie," he crooned. "I'm a friend of your daddy's." He held his hand out, and she sniffed it, coming closer. He tentatively scratched her ears, and her long tail started wagging. "Is your daddy okay? I'm real worried about him."

"Wyatt is fine. Who the fuck are you?" The female voice came from behind him. He felt the end of a phaser bump the back of his head. Fuck. He should be afraid, but he seemed stuck on the woman's first words. Wyatt was fine. Relief filled him even as the phaser pressed harder against his head.

"Who are you?" the woman asked again.

"My name is Morgan. The GACP sent me and my team to find its missing medical unit. Three of them are dead in the village. I'm searching for the remaining five. I'm guessing you're Kiki."

"Why do you think that?"

"I read your profile. You're very well trained, and I didn't hear you coming." He twisted quickly and grabbed the gun from her hand. "I'm well trained too though."

The woman had another phaser in her hand in seconds, but he didn't mind. He recognized her from her file. He also remembered she was married to a nurse on the team, Joe. One of the dead in the village. The picture in her file had been of a smiling woman, happy and content with life. He didn't know her, but he felt a stab to his gut at the loss of that woman.

"Joe's body is back in the village," he said.

"I know," she said, voice hoarse. "This has been the first time the area has been empty. I was going to bury them."

"I have two other people with me and a shuttle full of supplies. What do you need?"

"Supplies? They need food and medical supplies as soon as possible." She seemed to hesitate, and she looked back at the village. "We should get those first. I can bury him later."

"Okay," he said softly. "Are the others alright too?"

"Yeah," she said. "There are some injuries, but the most seriously wounded are the surviving villagers."

He pulled his comm out. "Garen, Quinn. I've found the survivors. Meet me back at the shuttle as soon as possible."

"*Yes!*" Quinn cheered. "On my way."

"I found some soldiers headed west," Garen said quietly. "They are headed away from the village, but they look to be searching for the ship. I'm heading back now."

"Garen," Morgan said. "Just so you know, Jane is okay."

The comm was silent for a minute. "Thank you," Garen whispered. "Thank you so damn much."

"Let's go find them," he said, snapping the comm closed.

Kiki and Luna fell in beside Morgan as they jogged back to the shuttle. "How do you know Wyatt?" Kiki asked. "You said you were a friend of his."

"Well, I am his friend. He just doesn't know me yet," he said as they arrived back at the shuttle. Quinn and Garen were leaning against it.

"Are you talking about Wyatt?" Quinn asked. She looked at Kiki. "He has a massive crush on the guy and hasn't even met the poor man."

"How do you know about my crush?" Morgan frowned at her as he opened the shuttle door for Luna.

"Everyone knows," she said, shrugging. "Alois messaged everyone. Even Selene and Leti back home."

"Fuck," he moaned, starting the shuttle. "That's just embarrassing."

Kiki watched him carefully, lips twitching. "Why do you like him so much?"

"He's adorable and sweet and kind and smart. I read his file and ran a background check myself," Morgan said, sighing. "He's delicious."

"Stalker," Garen coughed into his fist. Morgan

glared at him, but he just blinked innocently. "What? My throat had a tickle."

He followed Kiki's instructions, and they arrived at the cave system quickly. Unfortunately, a small troop of Concord mercenaries were firing at the entrance. One man crouched behind a large rock, firing back at them.

Morgan recognized him as Rune. He could hear cries coming from inside, and the mercs were approaching the cave fast, shields absorbing Rune's shots.

"Garen, stay in the shuttle with Luna," Morgan said.

The man grabbed the dog and held her tightly. They didn't need her running about in the middle of a fight.

Morgan looked back at Kiki and Quinn, smiling widely. "Let's have some fun, ladies."

yatt covered Estella and pressed them both against the wall at the entrance of the cave. Everyone was pushed against the sides, trying to stay out of range of the phasers the soldiers were firing into the cave. The shots hadn't hit anyone yet, but the cave entrance's covering disappeared, piece by piece. Their illusion of safety went with it.

"What are we going to do?" Panic filled Jane's voice, and Wyatt didn't know what to say. What could they do?

The foliage covering was completely gone now, and Wyatt could see the soldiers approaching through the heavy rain. Rune fired on them, but he was just one person, and they had personal shields.

A shuttle pulled up behind the soldiers, and Wyatt knew it was over. They must have called for reinforcements, or worse, that creature.

Then he saw him.

The man stepped out of the shuttle, a shield

covering him with a soft, blue light. He drew a large vibro-sword and launched himself into the line of soldiers. Wyatt barely noticed Kiki and another woman enter the battle too. His eyes were stuck on his hero.

The man cut a line through the soldiers, moving fast and efficiently. He twirled and jumped, dodging their attacks expertly. Wyatt's whole body seemed to vibrate and a loud hum filled his ears.

"Did time slow down, or is it just me?" Wyatt asked, watching the man dance through the soldiers, killing them.

"Wyatt? What's wrong? Are you okay?"

Jane's voice didn't register. Wyatt could think of nothing but his beautiful hero.

"He's so beautiful," Wyatt whispered.

"What the fuck?" Jane was trying to hold back desperate laughter. "What is wrong with you?"

"It's fine," Wyatt said. "He'll save us. Watch him move. Damn, he is so beautiful." He ran his hands through his hair. "I probably look even worse than normal, and I know I smell horrible. How's my breath?" He turned to Jane and huffed a breath in her face. "Well?"

"You've lost it. We're being rescued, and you finally lose it," Jane said. "Your breath is horrible too."

He gave her a wounded look. "Couldn't you have lied?"

Estella patted his shoulder from behind him. His sweet girl was always a comfort.

"The fighting has stopped," Jane said.

57

Pela rushed over to them before Jane had even finished her sentence.

Wyatt looked outside, and sure enough, his hero was putting away his vibro-sword. Kiki ran into the cave, eyes searching for wounded.

"No one was shot," Wyatt said. "You all arrived in time. Thank you, Kiki."

She looked relieved.

He pulled her over to their corner. "Who's that gorgeous man with you? Is he single? Do you think he might like me?" His face fell. "Never mind. I forgot I was pregnant." He rubbed his little bump.

Kiki tilted her head, looking just like Luna. "Did you hit your head?"

"He's been acting weird since he saw that guy," Jane said.

"He *is* handsome," Pela said, eyes wide in appreciation as she ogled Wyatt's hero.

"Back off, bitch," Wyatt said before he could stop himself. He looked at Pela, both of them shocked. "I'm so sorry, Pela. I don't know what's wrong with me." He shook his head, but his gaze got stuck on the tall blond again. "He makes the world vibrate and everything hum," Wyatt said dreamily.

"Vibrate and hum?" Kiki's eyes were soft, and she smiled sweetly.

"He's an idiot," Jane said, rolling her eyes. "Pela, I think you could take the Doc in a fight if it comes to it. Just saying." She looked at Kiki. "Now, are those people good guys?"

"They are," Kiki said. "The GACP sent them for us.

They have supplies in the shuttle, but we need to get out of here as soon as we can."

Wyatt shook his head. "Okay. Let's stabilize the most critical and give them whatever pain meds you brought. We can start moving the others. Where are we going?"

"There you are," Jane said, patting his cheek. "I'll go check the shuttle." She started for the shuttle, then froze. "Garen?" She screeched and launched herself into her husband's arms.

Luna trotted up and sat at his feet. She woofed hello. Wyatt bent and scratched her chin.

"Pela? Can you go check the shuttle for what medical supplies they have," Wyatt asked. "Jane is a bit preoccupied."

Pela grinned. "I can, and don't worry, Doc. I won't flirt with your man."

Wyatt growled as the nurse giggled and ran out of the cave.

Kiki patted his head. "Your growls aren't at all scary. Just cute."

He huffed. "Excuse me," he said. "I have patients to attend to."

He stuck his nose in the air and walked away. Estella followed suit, giving her own little huff.

He went to Rasha and her family first, Rune appearing at his side.

He smiled gratefully at his friend. "Rune, you did so well. Thank you for protecting us until they could get here."

"I thought we were goners," he said, face pale.

Dashel nodded in agreement. "Me too. Thank you, Rune. If you hadn't held them off, we would all be dead now."

Pela ran up with a box. "Here's a sample of what they have. Rune and I can start moving the most critical to the shuttle, and those that can could start walking back to the village. Kiki says we need to be fast."

"Good idea," Wyatt said. "Pela, if you'll tell Kiki to start directing them toward the village, Rune and I will begin getting the critical ready to move." He looked back at Rasha, giving her a grin. "We have the stuff to make you feel really good in here," he said, waggling his eyebrows. "Sit back and enjoy the ride, lady."

She smiled, eyes twinkling as her two kids giggled. "You're a sweet man, Doc."

"He really is." The deep voice behind him resonated up his spine, and he shivered.

Rasha watched him in fascination.

"Eep," Wyatt managed to say, turning to his hero. Up close, the man's brown eyes were even more fascinating then all his tattooed muscles. The man smiled at him, and Wyatt lost his mind.

He stared at the man, completely forgetting where they were as he plotted out their life together. They would have a whirlwind romance, then get married on Bella Torania in a beach-themed wedding. His mom and stepdad would love him, and of course his mom would cry at the wedding. They'd move to a nice planet and settle down. He'd get a job at a hospital, and his love could be a stay-at-home dad for their eight children.

He frowned. "Is eight children too many?"

"For what?" The man looked puzzled but kept smiling.

Rune and Dashel started laughing, and Wyatt blushed.

"Nothing," he said gruffly and held out his hand. "Sir. Thank you for your help."

It was time to turn on his doctor face.

The man raised an eyebrow but took his hand to shake. "My pleasure. I'm Morgan, by the way. No need for the *sir*."

"Nice to meet you," Wyatt said, face severe. "I'm Dr. Wyatt Morrick of the GACP. I'm not sure what's wrong with those two, but we truly are thankful."

The other two men just laughed harder, and Wyatt started to squirm.

"We should get to work here, gentlemen," Wyatt said finally.

"Sounds good," Morgan said. "Kiki is already on the way back with those who can walk. We'll start loading up when you're ready."

"Perfect," Wyatt said, nodding and keeping his serious doctor face in place.

"I will need my hand though," Morgan said, lips twitching.

Wyatt looked down to where he'd laced their fingers together, holding the other man's hand tightly in his.

"Oh, fuck," he said, letting go. "I'm so sorry."

Morgan grinned, and Wyatt's heart just about beat out of his chest. "No problem, kitten. You can hold my hand anytime you want."

Wyatt watched Morgan walk away, admiring his tight rear and the breadth of his shoulders, his long hair wrapped in a bun at the top of his head. Wyatt wondered what it would look like spread out on a bed.

Laughter broke through his thoughts, and he turned around to frown at the two men causing such a ruckus.

He propped hands on his hips and noticed Estella do it too. Smart little girl. "That's enough out of you two," Wyatt said. "We have work to do."

He turned his attention to Rasha, giving her a high dose of pain medicine.

"I think eight kids is a bit much," Rasha said as he worked on her injuries. The pain meds made her voice slur. "You should aim for four. That's a good number."

Wyatt blushed and hid his smile. "Was I a complete idiot?"

"No," Rasha replied, smiling. "You were adorable. He likes you. I could see it in his eyes."

"It doesn't really matter," Wyatt said, reminding his heart to be realistic. "I'm four months pregnant with another man's child. I can't pull anyone into that."

"If he's a man worth having, he won't care about that," Dashel said, squeezing his wife's hand. "He'll just care about being there for you and the baby."

"If he's a smart man," Rune said, handing him a fresh bandage. "He'll realize how dear you are and give you the eight kids you want. When I meet my fella, you can bet your ass I'll give him whatever he wants."

"Eight kids," Rasha said, drifting off to sleep. "That's too many little brats."

Her two little brats giggled at their mom's words, and Dashel smiled. "Is she ready to move?"

Wyatt finished with the last bandage. "Yes. You two be careful and keep a steady hand, okay?" He looked at the two little ones. "You two go with them and sit with Mama, alright? Hold her hands so they don't get cold."

Rune and Dashel lifted her cot and headed for the shuttle, the two little ones right behind them.

"Come on, Estella," he said. "On to the next patient."

$\mathcal{W}$yatt looked around his old office, Luna at his side. The village's medical rooms had been ransacked, and his belongings had clearly been checked for valuables. He knew better than to bring anything more valuable than his tablet with him, and he kept it on him at all times.

Too bad Ralen had cut their connection to the rest of the galaxy. Once they got off the planet, Wyatt imagined Gina would be able to fix it.

He looked out his window and watched the villagers gather their dead. The Tammolians burned their dead, and Kiki had decided to include Joe with them. Lolani and Ron would be brought back to their families.

Wyatt's chest felt heavy as he watched the people he had grown close to mourn their slain family members and friends. He looked to his own little shadow.

"Estella," he said. "Do you want to find your parents? We can take care of them together."

The little girl held tight to his hand. She hadn't let him go since they arrived, and Wyatt found he didn't want her to. She nodded and tugged him back out into the rain. Wyatt had only seen the little girl around the village a few times before the attack. He and his team had focused on the wounded.

She brought him to a little house near the center of the village and opened the door. Wyatt and Luna followed her inside. She squeezed his hand tightly as they walked through the living room and into the kitchen. Her mother had been killed by the creature and now lay as a husk on the floor.

Estella buried her face against Wyatt's belly, sobbing. Wyatt couldn't stop his own tears even if he'd wanted to. So much death.

"Need some help?"

Wyatt's heart lightened a bit at the sound of Morgan's voice, and he looked behind him.

"Please. This is Estella's mom. We need to get her properly buried. I think her dad is outside. He was one of the villagers who stayed behind to distract them while we escaped."

"I'll take care of it, kitten," Morgan said softly. He knelt next to the woman and gently picked up her hand. He slid the wedding ring from her finger and unhooked a necklace from around her neck. He held them both out to Estella. The little girl watched him with watery eyes, finally reaching out to take them.

"Sweetheart, I know this is hard. Believe me. I've been exactly where you are. I'll take care of your family, okay? Go pack some of your things. I don't know when you'll be able to come back. Pack everything you can't go without, pictures and anything else you can think of," Morgan said.

Estella let go of Wyatt and edged around her mother's body. She headed farther into the house, and Wyatt went with her, leaving Morgan to take care of the woman. The two of them worked their way through the house, and Wyatt made sure to grab anything he thought she might want later.

Her mom had made several quilts, and her dad apparently liked to carve. There were little wooden figurines all over. They ended up with three boxes of items sitting in the middle of the living room, and the little girl now hugged a stuffed bear-like animal to her chest.

"Estella," Morgan said from the door. The man was a muddy, soaked mess. "Your dad and mom are with the others now. Do you want to say goodbye?" He handed her another ring and a leather bracelet. She took them, lip trembling, and nodded.

Luckily, the rain had stopped. The sun shone through, making every puddle and drop of water gleam. As they walked to the edge of the village, Wyatt deftly slid Estella's parents' rings onto the chain of her mother's necklace. He stopped her and hooked it around her neck. It hung down to her chest, but she touched it gently, sniffling, and grabbed his hand again.

Estella handed Morgan her stuffed mystery animal and took the man's hand in her free one, startling him. Together, they found the others.

The village had a funeral pyre, but it had been

extended so everyone would fit. Wyatt stopped next to Dashel. His brother and parents had both died in the attack.

Kiki stood on the man's other side, and the Tammolian took her hand, surprising her. The woman on Kiki's other side grabbed her other hand, and one by one, they circled the bodies, hand in hand.

They watched the eldest of the Tammolians set the line of bodies on fire. Whatever accelerant they used was good. The wet bodies burned fast.

The elder began singing a song. It was in native Tammolian, so Wyatt couldn't understand the words, but he knew what it was about. He could hear the sorrow and pain. The others joined in, and the survivors mourned.

They were used to violence and death, but not at this scale. Not with this careless cruelty. He sobbed alongside them. He mourned Kiki's soulmate and Estella's parents. He mourned Lolani and Ron and what could have been. He mourned every brave villager who had stayed behind to save their loved ones.

When the bodies were ashes and bones, their song ended. One by one, the villagers said their goodbyes and melted away from the circle. Dashel squeezed Wyatt's hand and let go, turning to go back to his wife.

Wyatt scooted closer to Kiki, Estella pressed against his side and dragging Morgan with her.

Kiki stared at the pile a long time. "Did you know Havenites can sense their soulmates?" she asked. Joe had been a Havenite.

"Yeah," Wyatt said. "Both my mom and dad have Havenite blood. We're true galaxy mutts. No offence, Luna," he said, patting the dog's head. She perched between him and Kiki.

"The night Joe and I met, he told me that I made his world pulse. That he heard the universe strum and purr to him that he'd met his soulmate."

"Kiki," Wyatt said, voice cracking.

"I always thought humans didn't have life mates," she said. "We're plain and ordinary in all other ways. We do, Morgan. We do." She looked at the soldier, eyes red and aching, before turning to Wyatt. "You said that when you saw Morgan, the world seemed to vibrate and hum. Right?"

"Kiki," Wyatt said, embarrassed. "Don't mock me."

"He's your mate, Wyatt," she said softly, looking back to Morgan. "I know he is." She turned away and strode towards the shuttle.

Luna gave him a look and he nodded. The dog trotted after her.

Wyatt couldn't make himself look at Morgan. Fingers on his chin tipped his head up.

Morgan looked sad. "I feel bad for Kiki," he said. "She deserves more than this. They all do." He was quiet for a moment, fingers stroking Wyatt's chin. "Did the world really vibrate, Wyatt?"

"Yes," Wyatt admitted. "I saw you fighting in the rain, then the world vibrated and a hum filled my head. Now my heart's gone. Crazy, right? It happened so fast. My parents never had soulmates. I never thought I would. Don't worry though. I don't expect anything. You don't know me."

"I feel like I do," Morgan said. It started to rain again, and he raised his face up to meet it. "I have something to tell you and I really don't want to." He met Wyatt's stare again.

"It's okay. You can tell me."

"The GACP hired us to find you, but we were already looking. Your father got caught up in some trouble and hired the Charybdis mercenary group to help."

"That doesn't sound like Dad at all. What trouble could he come across at his lab?"

"Apparently, the owners and management of the lab weren't great people. They allied with the Concord mercenaries, the same people I fought today."

"What? Why are they here?" Wyatt asked.

"The Concords have decided to set up a base, and they chose Tammol to do it. They hate any non-human species. It's our understanding that they want to wipe them out."

"My dad's bosses work with them?"

"Yeah. It gets a lot more complicated though. This artifact came into your dad's possession. He was studying it but hadn't had much luck in figuring it out. He decided to work with Charybdis Station's scientists to try to understand it, but his bosses didn't like that. They had already agreed to hand it over to the Concords."

"What does the artifact do?"

"We don't know yet. We have people working on it, but so far, no one is sure what it is."

"That must piss Dad off. He hates not knowing something."

"That's what I really don't want to tell you," Morgan said, stepping close. "While we were trying to get him to safety, your dad was killed. He's dead, Wyatt."

"No," Wyatt said, shaking his head. His dad wasn't dead. He couldn't be. He was always there, focused on his work. "You're lying. Why would you do that?" He pushed Morgan away from him. "Why would you say that?"

He tried to turn and walk away, but Estella held his hand, tears streaming down her face and feet planted in the ground.

"It'll be okay, Wyatt," she said, voice hoarse from disuse. "I'm here with you."

She hadn't spoken in two months, and it broke his heart that she spoke to comfort him. Because his dad was dead. His dad died thinking Wyatt hated him.

He fell to his knees and hugged Estella to him, crying into her shoulder. She wrapped her thin arms around him, offering him the comfort that he'd given her countless times over the last two months.

The rain fell hard, and he was so damn cold. Then, he felt warm, strong arms wrap around them from behind. Morgan settled against him, murmuring nonsense against his back. Wyatt leaned back into him, pulling Estella with him, and cried.

WYATT WATCHED the ship come to a stop. It hadn't been able to fly too high, but at least it flew fast. The critical patients were taken straight to the medical bay, Jane and Pela with them, and Wyatt knew he needed to follow them.

His feet seemed stuck. He didn't want to think or feel. He didn't want to do anything. Estella stood beside him, and together, they watched Morgan direct everyone to either the ship or the shuttle. They had to leave here quickly.

Kiki stopped next to him, grabbing his hand. He felt a shove from behind and looked over his shoulder. Rune's sad eyes told him that they knew about his father.

"I know it hurts and you want to stop for a minute, Wyatt, but you don't have that luxury," Kiki said. "These people need you. Estella needs you." She nodded toward the girl. "We all need you, Wyatt."

"You aren't alone," Rune said. "We have each other, and we need you to stay with us."

"Okay," Wyatt said. "I need to move. I do." He headed for the ship, then stopped. "We need to get Estella's boxes and my bag."

"Morgan's already loaded them up," Kiki said. "Your shit went in his room. So did Estella's."

"What?"

"That got him moving," Rune said with a chuckle as Wyatt hurried toward the ship.

"Morgan, why is my stuff in your room?" Wyatt stopped next to the huge man and frowned up at him.

"We're mates," Morgan said simply, then turned back to helping the surviving villagers.

"I... What the hell?" Wyatt said, out of words.

"Well, well, well." A tall hybrid woman with caramel-colored skin stood in front of him. A vexal newt perched on her shoulder, eyeing the four of them carefully. "Here's our little Wyatt. Already sharing a room with pretty boy." She shook her head, tsking at him. "First Hack, now Morgan. Our Blue Solace boys work fast. Except for Alois. He's an idiot."

A Dedril and a very large, homely human walked past, carrying boxes for an elderly Tammolian and his grandson. The Dedril stuck his tongue out at the woman. "Thanks, Captain."

"Come on, Dru. Leave the boy alone." The human bent and kissed the woman's cheek. "You know how stressful starting a relationship can be. Don't tease him."

The woman pouted and stomped her foot. "I like teasing."

The man remained unconvinced, his face serious and his eyes gentle.

"Fine," Dru said and sighed. "I *am* the captain, so I should act like it." She turned back to Wyatt and his friends. "Welcome to the Blue Sparrow. We may not be able to fly above a hundred feet, but we have running water."

---

9

*M*organ piled blankets and pillows on the growing nest in the corner of his room. He'd made three more nests around the room and knew his crewmates were doing the same thing with their own quarters. The newly-rescued medical team and Tammolians needed somewhere to sleep, and each room had a bathroom.

Estella was in the shower, and Dashel and his kids were already freshly showered and dressed, ready to go and get a hot meal for the first time in months.

The Tammolian man moved nervously from foot to foot, eyes darting around the room.

"We can't take your bed, Morgan. It seems wrong," he finally said.

"Don't worry about it, Dashel. Rasha will be able to leave the med-bay tonight, and she needs somewhere comfortable to sleep."

"Then we can let her, Wyatt, and the kids have the bed. I don't want to take your mate's comfort."

"Dashel, I really like you, but if I'm going to cuddle with someone on the floor, I want it to be Wyatt."

Dashel's kids giggled, and the man managed a smile. "Fine. Cuddle with your mate on the floor."

Estella finally left the bathroom. She wore fresh clothes and clutched the necklace hanging from her neck. Her belongings were stacked near their nest. Morgan had made sure the ragged stuffed animal was happily perched in the middle of all the pillows.

She smiled when she saw it and ran to the boxes to dig around for shoes. She held a brush out to him, and he did his best to tame her wild curls.

Dashel tried to help, but the poor girl somehow ended up with a black, curly beehive. He would have to show her his special conditioner after dinner.

"Are you guys ready to eat? I know Garen has been cooking up a storm in the commons," Morgan said as soon as they were all ready.

"Food," Estella said, longingly. "MREs do the job, but they taste like poop. Are we going to get Wyatt on the way?"

"We'll take him a plate on the way back. I don't think we'll be able to make him leave the med-bay for a while."

The halls were full of Tammolians. Morgan and Alois had assigned everyone a space, but they were enjoying the freedom to walk around and explore the ship. Garen and a few of the rescued manned a table, passing out overloaded plates.

The kids rushed forward, eager for a warm meal.

Dashel and Morgan herded them to a table once they had collected their plates.

"This is so good." Estella spoke through a mouthful.

"I'm glad to hear you speak again, Estella," Dashel said, smiling at the young girl.

She shrugged. "I didn't mean to stop talking. I just didn't have anything to say. At the time, it seemed like if I talked to anyone, it would make it real."

"I understand," the man said softly. "I've spoken to Rasha. We have a way to go to find safety, but we would like for you to become part of our family."

She smiled, pleasure filling her eyes. "Thank you, sir, but I have Wyatt. I'm going to be a doctor like him and save lives. He needs me, and I need him." She nodded firmly, then went back to stuffing her face.

"Well, we are here if you need us," Dashel said with a smile.

"Sir." A young Tammolian man approached their table, eyes focused on Morgan. "I'm sorry to bother you, but is there anything you can tell me about the rest of the planet? We've passed seven villages so far, and they were all destroyed."

"We don't know much right now," Morgan said. "When we tried to land on the planet, we found out it has heavy defenses. If I understand correctly, that wasn't true six months ago. There are a lot of questions we need answers to, and I'll be going out with the shuttle soon to scout. We'll let you all know what we find out."

"Thank you," the man said. "My name is Rua. I can help, if you need me. Please." His brown eyes were full of pain. "My parents and grandparents are all dead. It's just me, my sister, and my two little brothers now. Those people and that thing have to be stopped."

"Have a seat." Morgan pointed to a chair at the table. "Everyone keeps referring to a mysterious creature. I don't understand."

"Remember my mama?" Estella's eyes looked haunted, and Morgan wished he'd kept his mouth shut. "She was killed by the creature."

"The Concords have someone with them that looks human, but isn't," Dashel said. "The creature lays eyes on a person or a group of people and calls everything liquid in their body into its own."

"Wyatt is working on a way to kill it," Estella said. "As long as it's alive, this world will never be safe."

"A phaser to the head should fix it," Morgan said.

"During the attack, Kiki and several others shot it. A few managed head shots," Rua said. "It didn't even slow it down."

"Anytime it was injured, it seemed to instantly heal," Dashel said.

"That's impossible," Morgan said, shaking his head.

"Yet it happened," Dashel said. "The village would have fallen anyway, but that creature is why more didn't escape."

"It has to see you to kill you," Estella said. "I hid in the cabinets, and it didn't see me. Mama didn't have time to hide."

"It just walked through the village laughing and killing everyone it could see." Rua shivered. "Imagine if it was in one of the cities."

"I'll talk to Dru. We need to let people know what's happening here," Morgan said. It had been bad enough when the Concords were just normal speciesist assholes. Add in an unkillable murder monster and shit just got a whole lot worse.

After dinner, Morgan, Dashel, and Estella filled up plates for Wyatt and Rune, then headed for the med-bay. Morgan couldn't stop his laughter when he saw Wyatt and Rune dancing around Rasha's bed, singing some outrageous pop song. The woman sang along, bobbing her head.

"I didn't know dancing had healing properties," Dashel chuckled.

"Hey, Dashel." Rune grinned and winked. "It's a secret. Don't tell anyone." The nurse moved on to another patient, still humming under his breath.

Wyatt was frozen, wide eyes fixed on Morgan. "You saw that?"

"Your awesome healing dance moves are impressive, kitten," Morgan said, grinning. He was thoroughly enjoying the blush that was spreading across his man's cheeks.

"Oh dear," Wyatt said, hands on his cheeks.

"We brought you dinner, Wyatt," Estella said. She pushed him into a chair and held out a plate. "Make sure you eat it all. The baby is probably hungry. I brought a plate for Rune too." She rushed off to hunt down the nurse.

"I'm glad she's talking again, but she's *really* bossy," Wyatt said.

Morgan sat next to him and watched Estella push

Rune into a seat too. The hybrid nurse was a huge, scary-looking man, but he melted when the little girl put her hands on her hips and glared at him.

"She's a little scary," Morgan said.

Wyatt grinned proudly. "Yeah. She is." He started shoveling food into his mouth, moaning at the taste. "This is so much better than MREs." His plate emptied quickly, and Morgan knew he'd be making a trip back to the commons. Wyatt took a deep breath, then took his hand. "Morgan, I owe you an apology for earlier. When you told me about Dad, I was awful to you. I'm sorry. There's no excuse. I was upset, but that was no reason to take it out on you."

Morgan laced their fingers together, smiling softly. "It's no problem, Wyatt. You were upset about your dad."

"How did he die?"

"We were retrieving an artifact from Union Station. The Concords wanted it and your dad. It was really bad. There was heavy fire, and he jumped in front of another man to save him."

"Sounds like him," Wyatt said. "He wanted to help people. That's what his work was about, you know. Protecting people."

"Turns out Sebastian, the man he saved, was pregnant too."

"Like me?"

"Yeah." Morgan brought Wyatt's hand up and kissed it. "Just like you."

"Does he have a mate?"

"He didn't at the time," Morgan said. "A few weeks

later, he met Alois, and we all think he's his mate. The way they react when they're together is hilarious."

"Alois doesn't mind about the baby? Even if it's not his?"

"I don't mind a bit," Alois said, plopping into the chair on Wyatt's other side. He stretched his legs out and moaned as he wiggled his toes in his boots. "My feet are aching. I've gotten lazy."

"You were unconscious for a month and healing, asshole," Morgan said. "We need to work you harder."

Wyatt put his doctor face on and looked Alois over. "What were your injuries? Why were you unconscious so long?" He stood and pulled his scanner out. Morgan watched him, enjoying his serious, practical expression – his doctor face. No one looking at him now would expect to see him dancing around a patient and singing to them.

"Ugh," Alois said, groaning. "Do we *really* need to do this? Can't we go back to talking about my soon-to-be mate and baby? Before we crashed here, Sebastian messaged that we're having a girl. He's going to name her Nina, after his cousin."

"Nina?" Wyatt sat. "Dad's assistant?"

"Yeah," Alois said. "She was killed helping Morrick keep the artifact out of the Concords' hands."

"She was such a sweet woman," Wyatt said, sinking back into his seat. "I talked to her weekly to check up on Dad. She made sure he ate and got some sleep."

"You kept tabs on him?" Alois watched Morgan's man curiously. "I know Morrick thought you didn't want to talk to him ever again."

Wyatt closed his eyes, lip trembling. Morgan reached behind him and smacked Alois's head. The man winced and mouthed *sorry*.

"When I was sixteen, he called me, wanting to spend some time together. It was the first time he'd ever called me without Mom making him. I was so angry. I told him it was too late, and I meant it at the time. That never stopped me from loving him."

"Fuck. Being a teenager is a hard thing anyway. Add in daddy issues, and it's even worse," Alois said. "I know he never gave up on you. When we get off this planet, you need to talk to Leti. He was Morrick's friend. He's also the one who's been messaging you with copies of your dad's letters."

"He sent some with us," Morgan said.

"I'll look at them," Wyatt said, eyes tired and sad. "Soon."

"You need to get some rest," Alois said. "And a shower. You stink."

"You're such a gentleman," Wyatt said, smiling. "You really don't mind that little Nina isn't yours?"

"Not a bit. I know Sebastian is meant to be mine. That means that little girl is meant to be mine too."

"When is the baby due?"

"In about four months," Alois said."

"Me too," Wyatt said. "That's funny, isn't it?"

"The Dedril don't believe in coincidences," Alois said. "I think you and Sebastian are meant to be best friends."

Wyatt shook his head. "You're a dork," he said. "You can't just find a best friend for your mate."

"You mean like I just did?" Alois gave him an innocent look. "Just like that."

"Doctor," Rune interrupted, voice grave. "We have a patient that needs another dance routine." The little girl in the bed he stood beside watched Wyatt hopefully.

Wyatt climbed to his feet. "If you'll excuse me, gentlemen, I have important doctor things to do."

A FEW WEEKS LATER, Morgan curled around Wyatt in their nest. His mate was freshly showered and dressed in a pair of Morgan's pajamas. Wyatt's small belly had outgrown most of his own pants, so he'd be wearing Morgan's sleep pants until they could find something better.

Morgan smiled, happy his kitten was wearing his clothes. Damn, he wished they were alone. Time had passed so quickly, and he was only just now realizing that they hadn't had any time to talk.

Estella and Luna were on Wyatt's other side, and several people shared their room, but that didn't lessen the peace Morgan felt holding his man.

He had so many more people to worry about now – Wyatt, Estella, the rest of the medical team, the surviving Tammolians, and he couldn't forget Luna. He smiled, nuzzling the soft, clean curls atop Wyatt's head. Morgan didn't give a damn. His ulcers could just suck it.

Of course, Wyatt said he didn't have ulcers.

Morgan's sexy little doctor had been concerned when Dru joked about his responsibility ulcers and insisted on examining him. Wyatt said it was just stress messing with his stomach, but Morgan knew that couldn't be right. He was good under pressure. There was no way he had an upset tummy due to stress. At least he would never admit that to Dru.

Morgan's comm beeped, and he quietly extracted himself from their nest and tiptoed to the hall, shoes in hand. "Yeah?"

"We just got a call from Jody," Dru said. "We're meeting in the conference room."

"On my way," he said, slipping his shoes on.

"I'm coming too," Kiki said from behind him.

Morgan jumped. "Fuck, Kiki. How are you so damn quiet?" She was sharing a corner nest in his room with Rune and Pela.

The woman shrugged, granting him a half smile. "You read my file." The redhead had trained with some of the best warriors in the galaxy. The GACP only hired the galaxy's finest, that was for sure.

"Come on," he said, leading the way.

"Who's Jody?"

"She's Lerais's sister and the head of the Foxtail Mercenaries."

"I've heard good things about them," Kiki said. "Wish I could say the same about the Concords."

"I know what you mean," Morgan said. "The Concords are the largest mercenary group in the galaxy, but at least they're not the best."

82

"With that creature on their side, the game changes."

"Fuck. Good point," Morgan said, disturbed at the thought of the creature. He was almost afraid to see the damage it had done to the planet.

10

They reached the conference room at the same time as Quinn and Linc. The shiny, gold hybrid rubbed sleep from her eyes. "Hazel is on guard duty," she said. Dru had decided to keep the ship moving during the day and park it in a secluded area at night.

So far, it seemed to work well. They tried to stay to the south, which was less populated. Unfortunately, they had yet to find any other survivors.

Dru sat at the head of the table, eyes troubled. Monty perched on Lerais's shoulder tonight. His little face was buried against the man's neck.

"What's going on?" Alois sat beside him, shirt half open, revealing the red scales on his chest.

"Jody managed to get a call through. The planet's defenses are insane. She can't get a ship through to us. She can't even do a scan of the planet. She's also afraid to stay close to the planet's surface for too long, so we'll get a short call each day."

"No supplies coming then?" Quinn pulled her hair back, tying it at the nape of her neck.

"No," Dru answered, face grim. "We can send out small groups to forage during the day. That will add to our resources. I spoke with some of the Tammolians earlier today, and they know the terrain well. Dashel and Rua will take out a small group each to look for food every day."

"Can we repair the ship without more resources?" Linc's nose twitched in worry, and his ears were pressed against his head.

"No," Lerais said. "Too much damage was done to even rig something together. Sometimes I wish I was Beck. He'd think of something."

Dru rubbed his shoulder. "Don't be stupid."

"We can go salvaging," Morgan said. "We have two shuttles. We can send one west, to one of the larger cities, and the other can work on searching for more survivors."

Dru nodded. "Alois, take a shuttle to search for survivors. Focus on areas within a few miles of a village." She looked thoughtful. "As for the city search, our readings showed more people to the north, so the west is the safer bet. We can establish a pre-set meeting place since we'll need to keep the ship moving during the day."

"Did Jody get word to the Lord Admiral?" Alois asked. Morgan knew he was more concerned with getting word back to Sebastian.

"She called him as soon as she lost contact with us and updated him on the situation. He sent some ships from each of the generals' fleets to help us, and he's sending the Yellow and Green Generals to different systems to start actively fighting the Concords. They've already fought off one attack near the station, so he's afraid to send out too many," Dru said.

"What's the plan long term? What if we can't find the parts to fix the ship? What about the Tammolians?" Morgan wished he was back in his nest with Wyatt.

Dru's worried face slowly shifted to a grin. "Jody is gathering a fleet of her own. Two other mercenary groups have already agreed to join with her against the Concords, and she's in the middle of talks with four more. Reggie leaked a bit of information, and the media got wind of Uncle Jevio's connection to the Concords and what's happening here. Let's just say most of the mercenary groups don't care for the idea of the Concords' plan to *purge* the galaxy. Between Charybdis Station's governmental shift, the Concords' recent actions, and Jody's personal connections, several mercenary groups are thinking about allying with us."

"Fuck. That's awesome," Alois said.

"What's that mean for Tammol?" Linc asked.

"I don't know," Dru said with a sigh. "We'll know more tomorrow after we do some scouting. I have a bad feeling that Tammol already belongs to the Concords. We can take it back, but based on what we've seen, how many Tammolians will be left?"

"We also told Jody about what's happened to Wyatt's team. She said she'll report it back to the GACP. They'll have more leverage against Ralen Jevio," Lerais said.

Kiki's laughter held a bitter edge. "There won't be any justice there. His family is too influential on Rueal."

"There are more ways to find justice," Lerais said. "This trial will be a thorn in his family's side and definitely hurt their reputation. Jevio, though, he'll get what's coming to him."

"Both Jody and Charybdis Station have friends within several assassin guilds, Kiki," Dru said. "I'll personally pay to make sure he dies for the deaths he caused."

"Why would you do that?" Kiki's eyes were wet with tears and pain. "Why would you do that for us?"

Dru was quiet for a minute, choosing her words carefully while everyone stared at her. Morgan knew Dru. He knew what was in her heart and why she was made captain. He knew what she saw as her responsibilities.

"Two reasons," Dru said. "First, like most back home, Charybdis Station took me in when my family tossed me out. Every single person on that station is my friend or my family. Morgan is an annoying ass, but he's my brother and Wyatt is his mate. That makes him mine, and that man loves you, Kiki. You and Wyatt have worked together for six plus years. I will make sure the man who hurt both of you pays with his life."

"What's the second reason?" Kiki asked, voice cracking.

"Charybdis Station does *not* stand back when it can help. That's the whole damn reason we declared war on the Concords. I personally won't stand aside if Jevio walks. Our new government may not be able to order an assassination, but I sure as hell can," Dru said.

Lerais nodded. "Jody will keep an eye on things while we're stuck down here. She knows what needs to happen."

Kiki smiled, relief and sadness holding equal parts in her eyes. She took a deep breath. "That just leaves the Concords' creature to deal with. So far, I've seen it immediately heal from a shot to the head and heart, a grenade blast, and a shot from a plasma cannon. We could try decapitation, but we'd be dead before we got close enough."

"I believe you—I do—but damn, that's insane," Lerais said, shaking his head. "A monster that drains its victims is like something from a horror movie."

"Estella said something about Wyatt coming up with a way to kill it," Morgan said.

"He's created a poison," Kiki said. She pulled a handwritten list from her pocket. "These are the ingredients he needs. Between the villages I visited and what you all have, I've gathered all but three things. One of the cities will likely have them."

"We're going to the west to salvage anyway, right?" Morgan scanned the list, noting the ingredients needed for the poison.

Dru thought for a moment. "Right, this is what we're going to do. Morgan, tomorrow morning you and I will take Kiki and Hazel to the western city. Dashel and Rua will lead groups to forage the woods to the east. Alois, again, you take a shuttle and check any villages you come across. Take Quinn with you just in case. Everyone needs to check in every thirty minutes. We'll meet at the large waterfalls to the south. I'll get you the exact coordinates." Dru paused. "Linc, you will keep the ship camouflaged and moving constantly. You're my contact to the ship, so watch communications. Lerais, baby, work on the ship. If you find anything else you need, message us."

The meeting broke up, and Morgan gladly headed back to his room and Wyatt. He curled behind his kitten, heart and stomach settling, and slept.

"YOU WILL BE CAREFUL, RIGHT?" Wyatt stuffed some sandwiches and medical supplies into their bags. "Kiki, please keep an eye on him."

"I'll watch your mate's back," Kiki said, tossing her loaded bag into the backseat of the shuttle.

"Morgan," Wyatt said softly, pulling his face down to whisper in his ear. "Watch out for Kiki too, please? She looks like a big tough guard, but she's vulnerable right now."

"You got it, kitten," he said, kissing Wyatt's forehead, making the man blush bright red. They were mates, had slept in each other's arms countless times, but they had yet to kiss. They'd get there when Wyatt was ready. Until then, Morgan took every chance to touch his man.

Luna ran and hopped in the backseat of the shuttle, wiggling between Kiki and Hazel. Wyatt sighed. "Luna, you can't go." The dog ignored him, eyes forward.

"She's a good scout," Kiki said, petting the dog's ears. "We'll leave her in the shuttle, Wyatt."

"Okay. Dru, keep them alive, alright?"

"You got it, Doctor Do-Good," she said with a wink, leaping into the driver's seat.

Morgan sat in the front and watched Wyatt until they were out of sight, then turned around, double-checking his shields and weapons. "What's the plan for the city?"

"Assuming it's not swarming with Concords, Hazel and I will look for the ship parts," Dru said. "You and Kiki will hunt up the ingredients for the poison. We also need to record as much as possible. We need to know what the Concords have done to the planet. Ideally, we'll find a city full of healthy Tammolians."

Morgan used his comm to record their approach to the city. According to their information on the planet, Synegana was the third largest city on the planet with an average population of just under four million.

Now, the city was in shambles and surrounded by the Concords. Crashed shuttles littered the roads surrounding the city, and Dru lowered their own behind a pile of shuttle parts in the forest. Morgan swallowed when he saw a dried, shriveled hand peeking out of the pile.

They unloaded and looked around. Luna followed Kiki as she peeked into an almost intact shuttle. "If Synegana has already fallen, the other cities probably have too," Kiki said. "The planet only has five large and two smaller cities. The rest are villages."

"They look like they were just going about their business," Hazel said, eyes scouring the woods.

"Based on the state of the corpses, it's been a good four months," Dru said, eyes pointing to the three corpses in one crashed shuttle. "I'm not an expert though, and they're not normal corpses."

Morgan took a picture and sent it to Wyatt. Seconds later, he got a reply. "Wyatt says it looks more like two and a half months. Exposure makes it look worse."

"That fits with the timeline," Dru said. "They attack the cities, then move out into the villages." She shook her head. "Come on. Let's sneak into the city and find what we need. This won't be easy, but it has to be done."

Kiki pointed to the shuttle, and Luna reluctantly crawled back in, disappearing. "She's used to being my scouting partner, but we need to be extra stealthy."

"Stay in contact with me. Buzz in every fifteen minutes," Dru said. "Hazel and I are going to fly over to the other side of the city where the spaceport is. We meet back here in two hours, whether we've found what we need or not."

Morgan nodded, and Kiki and he quickly moved toward the city walls, sneaking over and in between Concord patrols. They ducked into the remnants of a building, watching the Concord shuttles fly by.

He recorded the perfectly intact buildings on his comm, zooming in on the withered corpses and crashed shuttles in the street. There were hundreds obviously killed by the creature, and the Concords had just left them there. They were holding the city but hadn't had the time to clean it out and make it their own.

Morgan and Kiki moved building to building, recording what they found within each one. "Something isn't right. Kiki, I thought someone said the creature had to see a person to drain them," Morgan said.

He couldn't bring himself to take a picture of the corpse sitting on the toilet. He went back into the living room. "Come to think of it, a lot of these bodies in the houses wouldn't have been visible to him unless he came in each one. That doesn't seem efficient, and it would have given people time to run."

"This doesn't make sense," Kiki replied, looking at the withered body of the cat sitting on the couch. "In the village, the creature killed some in the street but not all. Then he went in the houses, finding who he could. Why would he do that there, but basically drain the whole city at once here? Those people in the street weren't running. There was traffic in each direction."

"Fuck," Morgan said, thoughts dark. "In the village, he was having fun and letting the soldiers play."

"Here, it was more serious." She looked at him in horror. "He took out the whole city, didn't he? Every man, woman, child, and animal. Anything living."

"We can't know for sure, but that's my bet," Morgan said, looking around. "Come on. Let's find those supplies and get the fuck out of here."

They covered five miles before they found a pharmacy. They slowly moved in, surprised at the amount of goods still sitting on the shelves. Four dead Tammolians were scattered throughout the store. They had been going about their day when the attack happened.

Morgan recorded the scene in front of them as Kiki started bagging everything. "I'll be right back. I'm going to check the building next door too," he said. "The more footage we have, the better."

"Got it," Kiki replied. "I'll get everything we can carry from here. This should make Wyatt very happy."

Morgan moved to the other building, recording as he entered. It had been a small, neighborhood supermarket, and there were more dead Tammolians here. His heart broke as he recorded them. The husbands with their wives and children. The elderly couple that still held hands. The young enforcement guard with her phaser holstered.

He closed his comm and started gathering as much of the unspoiled food as he could. Lost in thought, he didn't hear the rustling right away. He was right next to the front counter when something darted out, climbing up his leg. He squealed and danced around, trying to shake the critter off. Whatever it was clung to him and hissed.

Laughter came from the door.

Kiki was doubled over, but her comm was still aimed at him. "Oh gods, you just squealed. Big, bad soldier boy just squealed."

"I'm being attacked," he said, squealing again when the animal climbed up his back. "Help."

She just laughed harder.

He finally got a hold of the animal and pulled it off his back by its ruff. He held it up, scowling. It had felt bigger climbing around on him. The critter was a smallish feline. To Morgan, it looked like a mix between an opossum and a housecat. He noticed the collar around its neck. It had been someone's pet.

"This is the horrid beast that attacked you?" Kiki's chuckles made him happy even if they were at his expense. The woman needed some good in her life.

"I think it was someone's pet."

"It's a Tammolian house cat," Kiki said. "It looks young. They usually get a lot bigger. I wonder how he survived. Maybe he came into the city looking for food."

"You aren't for me, but I know someone who wants a co-pilot pet, little beastie," Morgan told the cat. "What do you say?"

"Meow."

"Okay, then. I'll introduce you to Linc."

"Meow."

Morgan nodded and tucked the little terror under his arm. "I found a lot of food before I was attacked," he said, pointing to the pile of bags at the door. "I think that's all I can carry though. Did you find the ingredients?"

"Yes," she said. "Plus a lot of medication and other medical supplies. Let's get out of here. We have forty-five minutes to get back to the meeting spot."

She picked up her bags, and he grabbed his. Time to get moving.

They made it back to the spot, minutes to spare.

The shuttle was there, and Hazel and Dru hopped out to help him load it.

"Damn. You two did good," Dru said. "Were all the ingredients there?"

"Yeah," he said. "I got some recordings too. We can send them to Jody."

They all loaded up, and Luna sniffed at the cat.

"We got some video too. There were plenty of ships going in and out of the spaceport, including one passenger ship from Rueal with Jevio's uncle onboard," Dru said.

"There was also a huge pile of bodies," Hazel said, voice full of horror. "It was near the spaceport. It's like they just shoveled the bodies out of the building and to the side, then left them there."

"There were thousands of bodies, Morgan," Dru said, voice tired. "They were all dried up, like some of the corpses in the village."

"Every corpse we came across was like that," Kiki said. "The creature did the killing here. It's more dangerous than we initially thought. It was bad enough when we thought it could just instantly kill whoever it laid its eyes on, but it wiped out this whole city."

"It has to be stopped," Dru said quietly.

"Did you guys find the parts we need?" Morgan asked, petting the wiggling cat. They needed to kill the creature. That was something he was completely certain of. The Concords didn't need that weapon.

"We found the essentials," Hazel said. "It's enough to get us off the planet if the planetary defenses are down."

"Closer than we were," Morgan said, shrugging.

"What you got there, Morgan?" Dru asked, smiling as the cat batted at Luna.

"He was attacked by that vicious beast," Kiki said, laughter in her voice. "I got it on video."

"Perfect," Dru said gleefully. "I knew I liked you for a reason, Kiki."

11

"*D*oc, you need to take a break," Pela said. The young nurse became more and more steady each day. She still jumped when she was startled, but she was starting to get back to her sassy playful self. She grinned at him. "You could go find that hot man of yours and have some fun." She wiggled her eyebrows up and down. "He looks so tasty."

"Keep your eyes to yourself," Wyatt said, smacking her on the arm with his tablet. He wrinkled his nose. "I don't want to take a break. I'll have to be all adulty and write a message for my mom. How am I going to explain what happened without telling her I'm pregnant? If she knows that, she'll drag my stepdad and my little brothers to Rueal to ambush me when we leave here."

"You're a great big scaredy-cat," Pela said, shaking her head. "I know your mom. Sandra is a smart lady. She'll understand, and she'll spoil those babies of yours rotten."

"Babies! Bite your tongue."

She arched a brow. "You're the doctor. What do you make of your oversized belly? I mean, there could be other explanations, but it's looking like you're going to have multiples."

"You're a horrible, horrible woman," he said. "I'm going to take a break and try to forget everything you just said."

Back in his room, Wyatt finished the message to his mom but hesitated to send it. Everything was so complicated. His dad was dead, he'd lost some of his friends, he was pregnant, he had a new kid whether he liked it or not, and he'd found his mate.

What would she think about it all? His mom had loved his dad for a long time, even after they had divorced, and she'd left him to his work. Wyatt had thought she would never move on.

Then his stepdad had shown up about seven years ago. The man had managed to sweep his mom off her feet. Now, he had two new half-brothers and a stepdad. She was so happy now, and he didn't want to ruin it. He'd never disappointed her before.

He was afraid to tell her about the baby and Jevio, and despite what everyone said, this whole thing was his fault. He'd fallen for the first handsome man to pay him any attention and made some stupid choices.

Then there was Morgan. His beautiful Morgan. In the past two weeks, there had been no intimate touches or kisses, but damn did the man take good care of him. His belly had grown much larger since he had plenty of food, and he was more than a little worried.

Pela was right. His belly seemed a little too big. He had always been a bit lean, so it might just be natural to his frame, but he had a feeling it wasn't. He still couldn't make himself do the tests he needed to do, despite his friend's nagging.

He pushed aside his thoughts and his hesitation and sent the message to Dru, so she could upload it to Jody during their next talk. Being out of contact with the rest of the galaxy was frightening, but at least they weren't living in a cave now.

He swiveled in Morgan's chair, giggling as he spun in circles. He *had* needed this break from the med-bay. They finally had every critical patient stable and on the mend, but with daily foraging and scouting trips, there were always injuries to tend to.

"Here you are, kitten," Morgan said, walking into the room, Luna beside him. He carried a plate topped high with food. "I wondered where you'd gone off to. I brought you some lunch."

Wyatt made grabby hands from his seat. He could already taste the delicious food. Garen was a wonderful cook and had mastered some of the local dishes. Morgan laughed at him and handed over the plate.

"Thanks," Wyatt managed to say before digging in. Morgan pulled a chair from across the room to sit next to him. Wyatt thought his man looked too tired. "How did the scouting trip go?"

"Six more destroyed villages and no survivors. Dashel thinks that if there had been any survivors, they would have hidden like you all did," Morgan said.

"Does he know any of their hidey-holes?"

"No. Apparently each village keeps that information secret."

"What if there aren't any survivors?" Wyatt asked.

"There have to be," Morgan said. "I think they're just hidden away, which is probably for the best."

"On a lighter note, how's Nugget doing?" Wyatt stifled his laugh at Morgan's scowl. Kiki had shown him the video of Morgan being attacked by the Tammolian cat, and he'd laughed for days.

"Linc loves the little fucker. The thing hisses at me every time I'm around," Morgan said, clearly insulted. "I saved the damn thing from a lonely, dangerous life. You would think it could be a little less hissy."

Luna laid her head on Morgan's knee.

"Aww, Luna loves you. She'll be your girl," Wyatt said.

His dog had taken to following Morgan and Kiki around constantly. She was now an official scout dog.

Morgan sniffed, still pouting. "She *is* the best dog in all the galaxy." He petted her ears. "She's your dog though." He smiled sheepishly. "I kind of want my own pet. It seems like most of Blue Solace has at least one."

"One day, you'll meet something special," Wyatt said, snickering. "All it'll take is one look, and you'll know."

"Ha ha. Very funny. Anyway, I wanted to ask you on a picnic. Dashel told me about a hidden waterfall a few miles away. It should be safe enough, and hopefully, it's not full of slugs."

"Wow, that's so romantic," Wyatt said wryly. "I could use some time off the ship though. It's better than the cave, but I'd love to smell some fresh air. I just ate lunch though."

"You saying you aren't still a little peckish?"

Wyatt glared at the irritating man. "I could still eat," he finally admitted. "Where's Estella? She and Rasha were visiting with the patients when I left the med-bay." He missed his shadow.

"I made her go get some lunch. Let's go," Morgan said, excited. He pulled Wyatt out of the chair. "I have everything ready and waiting in the shuttle."

They held hands as they walked through the small ship's halls, and Morgan helped Wyatt into the shuttle. His mate was such a gentleman. Morgan slipped into the driver's side after letting Luna into the back, and they left the ship behind.

Wyatt watched the heavy forests of Tammol as they sped by. The planet was small, but it was so vibrant. The Concords needed to be stopped.

About ten minutes later, Morgan lowered the shuttle. "We'll need to walk the rest of the way," he said, leaving the camouflage shield activated on the shuttle. He helped Wyatt out, and they started the uphill walk.

"It's so nice to be outdoors again," Wyatt said. He peeked at Morgan from the corner of his eye. "So, Dru called me into her office for a *talk* a few days ago."

"Fuck. What did she say? You really shouldn't take her too seriously."

"She told me about your parents," Wyatt said.

Morgan rolled his eyes. "Why is she so concerned about my parents?"

"She seems to think this situation has brought back

some bad memories," Wyatt said. "She didn't really give me any details."

"I was born on Union Station. My parents owned a store in the lower city during the Gang Wars. In the past, they'd had good relations with all the gangs. They always stayed neutral. Then things started getting really bad. They sent me to stay with one of their friends for a few weeks, and they stayed behind to watch the store. They were murdered during the fighting," Morgan said.

"I'm so sorry you lost them, Morgan. I'm sorry you had to come here on top of that," Wyatt said.

"No," Morgan said. "No feeling guilty. First, I came to terms with my parents' deaths a long time ago. Dru is just taking her role as captain way too seriously and overanalyzing everything. Second, I'm so damn happy to be here. I found you, Wyatt, and that is the best thing to ever happen to me."

"Really?" Wyatt's grin had to look insane, it felt so big, and warmth filled him. Maybe he wasn't the only idiot to fall for someone so fast.

"Yes," Morgan said, squeezing his hand. "General Hackett was my former captain, and he found his mate a few months ago. I was so jealous, and I didn't know why. I never thought I'd want someone of my own. I was happy being single and a simple soldier with no responsibilities."

"What changed? I know you're my mate, but that can't be everything."

"It isn't just you, though that would be enough. It seems like everyone is settling down. My best friends,

Draif and Lucas, are dancing around each other. Draif is Lucas's mate, but he doesn't know, and Lucas wants to take his time. Then, there's General Hackett. He found Leti and adopted half the galaxy. My mentor, Selene, the woman who has been my family since I arrived at Charybdis Station, adopted a son. She's settling down now too. It just felt like it was my time," Morgan said. He gave Wyatt a warm look. "Then I saw your picture, and the thought of us together just fit."

"What if you hadn't met me? Would you just have found someone else?"

"No. I would have just been lonely until we eventually met," Morgan said, kissing Wyatt's hand. "Humans may not feel their soulmates like a lot of other species, but it doesn't mean we don't have them. Obviously." He gestured between the two of them. "I think it was just my way of getting ready for you. Now, we've met, so we can get to know each other and fall in love."

"I like that," Wyatt said. The knowledge that Morgan was his mate made everything so scary and difficult. If he messed up, he messed up big. He was ready to risk it though. He wanted to get to know the man and fall in love with him too much to be a scaredy-cat.

They walked in silence for a bit, both enjoying the peaceful scenery. "Have you read your dad's letters yet?" Morgan's voice was hesitant, and Wyatt didn't blame him. He had refused to talk about his dad for a while now.

"Not yet," he whispered. "I'm getting there. I never thought it would hurt so much to lose him."

"I get it. I was really close to my parents. When they died, they knew I loved them, and I knew they loved me. It hurt like hell, but Selene and my new parents helped me move on. I still miss them, but there's no unfinished business between us. I think that makes it worse for you."

"I do have unfinished business with Dad," Wyatt admitted. He made a face. "I'll deal with it."

"For now, let's enjoy the day. Look," Morgan said as they stepped into a clearing. He pointed at the beautiful silver and lilac waterfall. Luna ran into the clearing, stopping to sniff the ground along the way.

"This planet is so beautiful," Wyatt said breathlessly. "I hope we can get the Concords off it so the Tammolians can move on."

"We'll do it," Morgan said. "Jody's gathering her fleet." He spread a blanket out on the ground close to the pool. He set his basket down and looked around. "I bet you there are fish in there."

"Probably," Wyatt said, watching Morgan pace around. "You want to fish, don't you?"

"No," Morgan said, shaking his head, settling next to him. "We're here to have a picnic and get to know each other."

Morgan watched closely as Wyatt unpacked the basket and bit into a sandwich. Wyatt chewed slowly, as they stared at one another. "Why aren't you eating?"

"I already had lunch."

"Okay, you can't just sit and watch me eat," Wyatt said. "It's weird. Go fish or something."

"But…"

"I can learn a lot from your fishing techniques," Wyatt said in his proper doctor voice. "Show me your ways."

Morgan laughed and jumped up, pulling off his shoes and shirt. Wyatt licked his lips. Damn, that was a well-built chest. He polished off his sandwich and started on the diced fruit, which was native to the planet and yummy. Morgan pulled a fishing pole out of the basket and unfolded it.

"I'll catch us dinner, kitten," he said.

"You go, baby. Catch those fish," Wyatt buried his head in the basket, looking for more goodies.

Wyatt ate all the food, savoring it, and joined Morgan at the pond. They fished and talked quietly until the sun was sitting low in the sky.

"I can't believe you caught eight fish," Wyatt said, holding up his own tiny catch. He unhooked it and tossed it back into the pond. It was too small to be anyone's dinner.

"You caught three others, kitten," Morgan said proudly. "They're huge too. Plus, this was your first time fishing. I can't believe you haven't been before."

"It's been school, school, school, then work, work, work," Wyatt said.

"For me, it's mostly been fun, fun, fight, fight, fun, fun," Morgan said. "I can totally teach you fun."

Wyatt laughed. "I had fun at school and work."

"No," Morgan said, horrified. "No one has fun at

school and work. It's okay, kitten. I'm here for you." He hugged him tightly. "I'll teach you to have fun. I promise. I'll let you shoot at the trainees. That's a lot of fun."

"There's something wrong with you," Wyatt said, laughing against his chest.

12

_W_yatt helped Morgan pack up their blanket, smiling as his mate checked the fish in the cooler again. "Garen will do beautiful, beautiful things to you," Morgan told the fish.

"Put the lid on the cooler and come on, you weirdo," Wyatt said.

"Okay, okay."

"Put... Put the cooler down." A hesitant voice came from the trees. A young Tammolian man stepped out. He held a rusty phaser pointed toward them. The poor man looked malnourished and starving.

Morgan growled, but Wyatt stepped in front of him. "Of course," he said. "We caught eleven fish, and they're pretty big. I have some bread and a small pack of mustard left over in the picnic basket too." He looked around but didn't see Luna.

Morgan pushed Wyatt behind him again, glaring at him. Wyatt frowned but let his mate have his way.

"Put that down too, please," the man said. What kind of thief said *please*?

"My name is Dr. Wyatt Morrick. Are you from one of the destroyed villages?"

"*One* of the destroyed villages? They're all destroyed," the man said, grief thickening his voice.

"Is it just you?" Wyatt asked softly. The young man slowly moved closer.

"None of your business. You're not like the other off-worlders," the man said.

"I work with the GACP," Wyatt said. "My team and I were staying in Jarth. The village was attacked, and we managed to escape with several others."

"There are others?" The hope in the man's eyes just about broke Wyatt's heart. The man lowered his arm, and Morgan darted forward, grabbing the man's gun.

"*No*." Someone screamed from the woods, and a shot hit Wyatt's leg. Pain blossomed in his thigh, and his leg buckled. He fell to the ground, and Morgan went crazy.

Morgan twisted around, pulling the man in front of him and pointed his phaser against the stranger's head. "Stop firing or I'll kill him. You just shot my pregnant mate, you stupid fucker."

"I'm sorry. Please don't hurt him." The voice coming from the woods was young. Too damn young. "I gave the dog my gun." Luna walked out of the woods, a phaser in her mouth.

"Morgan, I think it's a child. Don't scare them," Wyatt said, trying to push his pain away. He pulled one of the cloth napkins from the basket and wrapped it around his leg.

"Don't scare them? They *shot* you," Morgan said. Wyatt looked up. His mate was pissed. His face was stone cold and his eyes full of rage.

"Morgan, I'll be okay. These people are survivors who have had their world ravaged. Think, baby, think."

"It's my little sister," the young man said. "She wouldn't stay with the others. I'm all she has."

"Make her come out here. I won't hurt you, but I can't risk my mate," Morgan said, gritting his teeth.

"Mayla, it's okay. These people aren't the soldiers that destroyed the village," the man called out. "They're scared though. Like us. Come out, so they know we aren't bad guys."

"You sure, Narin?" The girl's voice was doubtful.

"Positive," Narin said. "He said he was Dr. Wyatt. Remember what Mama said?"

"He made her broken ankle better."

"Yeah, sweetheart. Come on," Narin said.

A Tammolian girl came out from behind the trees. She couldn't be more than twelve and looked as ragged as her brother. Morgan pushed Narin away, and the brother and sister hugged, looking back at Morgan. They were at the man's mercy now. Morgan took a deep breath and holstered his phaser. Wyatt could feel his mate's rage crawl along his skin. He held out his hand, and Morgan was there, kneeling beside him.

"I'm going to be okay," Wyatt said. "I've slowed the bleeding. We need to help them, Morgan."

"How the fuck does Hack do this shit?" Morgan

turned to the Tammolians. "Okay. We have a group of survivors on our ship. You and anyone else who want to come are welcome. We have running water, medical supplies, and food."

"Food?" Mayla asked.

"It's delicious," Wyatt said.

"Who are the soldiers attacking our planet?" Narin's eyes were afraid, but he asked the right questions.

"They're a group of mercenaries, and we have friends who are trying to stop them. We didn't know what was happening on Tammol until we crashed here," Morgan said. "Okay. Here is what's happening. I'm going to get Wyatt back to the ship. Then, I'll bring the shuttle back here in an hour. Can you get the rest of your group here by then?"

"If they'll come, yeah." Narin didn't sound so sure they would.

"I'll bring my captain. If they want to talk to her before coming aboard, that's fine."

"Okay," Narin said, nodding.

Mayla knelt at Wyatt's side, tears filling her eyes. "I'm so sorry," she said. "I thought you were going to kill Narin."

"It's okay, sweetie," Wyatt said, reaching for her hand. "I understand, and I'm going to be fine."

"What about the baby?" she asked, voice low and worried.

"The baby isn't in my leg, so he or she should be just fine."

"Keep the cooler and basket," Morgan said. He wrapped the blanket around Wyatt and picked him up.

"I'll be back." He wasted no more time talking and started running toward the shuttle. Luna ran beside him. Wyatt hadn't realized a dog could look worried. He leaned up and kissed Morgan's clenched jaw. His poor mate.

Less than twenty minutes later, they were back at the ship, and Jane and Rune fussed over him in the med-bay. "Morgan, it'll be okay," Wyatt said. His mate wasn't moving from his side. "You need to get back to those people. Be careful, okay?"

"Careful? I shouldn't have taken you out there. I knew things weren't safe," Morgan said. "I'm the worst fucking mate in the galaxy. You deserve so much better."

"Don't be a jackass, Morgan Murray," Wyatt yelled, startling everyone in the room. "Only teenagers get to be angsty buttheads." He grabbed a handful of Morgan's shirt and pulled him down. "Never, ever doubt us."

Wyatt pressed his lips to Morgan's, aiming for a short, gentle kiss. Morgan's mouth had dropped open though, and he tasted so damn good.

Their kiss wasn't short, and it wasn't gentle. Morgan's tongue twisted around his own, and heat ran through him, from his toes to his ears.

When he finally released Morgan, his brain was too foggy for thinking. "Eight kids really wouldn't be too many," Wyatt said breathlessly.

Jane covered her face with her hand while Rune laughed. "You are so weird," she said.

Alois clapped Morgan on the shoulder. "If you can

bring yourself to think after that kiss, we need to go check on those survivors. Your mate is in good hands."

"Mm-hmm," Morgan said. His eyes were hot and ran up and down Wyatt's body.

"Come on, pretty boy. Leave Hot Lips there alone," Dru said, pulling Morgan away. "Get better fast, Doc. I have a feeling we're going to need you."

WYATT LAY in his nest in the corner of their room, leg propped up. Everyone else had left for their own chores, but he had reluctantly agreed to rest while his three nurses tended to the new group of Tammolians.

Three new nests were settled on the floor of Morgan's room, and Wyatt knew overcrowding was going to be a problem if this ended up being a long-term thing.

"How many did you say they had in the new group?" Wyatt's brain was foggy from the light dose of pain medication Jane gave him that morning. He never reacted well to it.

"I counted fifty-seven," Estella said. The little girl was curled into Wyatt's side, her head on his shoulder. "I think there are others out there, hiding. I hope they'll be okay until we can save Tammol."

"Me too," Wyatt said, trying to mentally catalog their medical supplies. His brain wouldn't work with him. "Blah, I can't think."

"Then rest," Estella said. "You need rest to get better."

"I'm not tired yet," he said, pouting.

"You are such a baby," she said, exasperated. Estella reached into one of their bags and pulled out his tablet. "Here. Play a game or something."

His tablet couldn't connect to anything off world and the Tammolian systems were down, but he had a lot of articles and books about Tammol saved to it. Plus, while he had already finished putting together the poison, it couldn't hurt to review his notes. He signed in and froze. He had almost forgotten that he'd downloaded his dad's letters. Morgan brought copies on his own personal device. Damn it. Maybe it was time.

Wyatt took a deep breath and pulled up the first one. He read it quickly, then reread it six times, cheeks wet with tears. He shook his head. This couldn't be right. He read the next, eyes hungry for his dad's words, for the cherished peek into his thoughts. Then he read the next letter and the next. Estella held him tightly, his head buried against her stomach. He sobbed as he read.

His father had missed his birth, missed all the family holidays and his birthdays, missed his honor shows and school awards ceremonies. These were things he knew. He'd lived them.

His dad had reached out once, yes, but Wyatt hadn't understood at the time. He hadn't known his father struggled with doubt and guilt, and that he thought of Wyatt almost every second of the day. He hadn't known his father adored him. He sped through the eleven letters, then reread the last one.

My beloved son,

I am an idiot. I understand viruses. I understand parasites and genetics. I understand quite a bit, but that isn't enough. I don't understand family, relationships, and love. I am your father, but I am utterly useless. I know I love you, but I cannot make myself show it. I cannot make myself tell you how wonderful you are. I helped make you, but aside from financial security, that is all I have ever given you.

Your mother left yesterday and took you with her. I wasn't even there. I know she left, because she called and left a message. I don't blame her, not one bit. She is an amazing woman and deserves more than me. You deserve more than me.

One day I will do better. I will be better. Tonight, I close my eyes and think about that future. You and I will sit on the couch and talk about school. I'll give you advice and help you understand that life is scary, but it is so exciting too. The possibilities in this galaxy are endless, and you are so smart, so creative. I cannot wait to see the man you grow into. I hope I can be there.

I love you more than all the stardust in the galaxy.

-- Your father

13

*M*organ stood with Kiki and watched the small group of volunteers as they ran through the third basic move of the day – the uppercut. In the past week, all of the sixty-two volunteers had improved in hand-to-hand combat drastically. The Tammolians had lost their planet, their homes, and their families. Now, the able-bodied wanted to fight.

"Pela, work on your stance," Morgan said. He watched the young nurse fix her stance and move back into the routine. Forty minutes later, he gave them a break. Kiki led a new group in.

He caught Pela before she left with the others, pulling her aside. "Pela, are you sure you want to be here?"

"I'm tired of being afraid," she said. "I know my training is medical, but I want to fight. I want to stop that thing."

"Pela, you don't have to be a soldier to fight."

"I know. I'm a field medic, Morgan. I've had it easy

until this post. I should have been better prepared," she said, looking at her feet. "I really liked Ron and Lolani. They were good people and were falling in love with each other. Now they're dead. All I did was run, and running won't protect my patients. It won't protect this world or any other worlds that thing could attack. My dads and my little sister live on Rueal. That's not too far from here. What if the Concords attack my home? Papa and Dad are both hybrids like Wyatt. The Concords want to kill non-humans."

"I understand you're afraid for your family, and the creature will die, I swear it, but you can help us more as a nurse, Pela."

"I'm proud to be a nurse, but I'll be proud to be a Charybdis soldier too," she said, chin in the air. "I can and will be both. The stories everyone tells about your home are amazing. I want to stand up and be strong too."

Morgan sighed and let her go. He felt worried for her and proud of her at the same time. He rubbed his stomach. Damn ulcer. The next class stood ready, and they started the more advanced routine.

"Morgan." Estella ran into the training room. "Wyatt needs you. He read his daddy's letters, and I can't get him to stop crying. He hurts so much," she said, tears falling down her own cheeks. "He helped me when I lost Mama and Daddy. Please, Morgan. We have to help him."

Oh damn. Morgan left the Tammolian volunteers without another thought, vaguely aware of Alois stepping in to continue their training.

Wyatt was curled into a ball in their nest, his injured leg sticking out, his small body shaking. Morgan couldn't bear to hear the sobs coming from his mate. He quickly curled behind him, mumbling nonsense in Wyatt's ear. Estella curled against Wyatt's front, her thin arms wrapped around his waist, and she hugged him tightly.

They rocked for minutes or hours, Morgan couldn't tell. Morgan barely noticed when Kiki and Rune joined them, piling into the nest. Slowly, Wyatt's tears slowed.

"I told him that he wasn't my father. That it was too little, too late," Wyatt whispered. "He loved me, adored me, and I just told him it was too late."

"Kitten, you didn't know," Morgan said, his own voice thick with tears. He wished he had spoken more with Verion Morrick when he'd had the chance. Leti was the only one who had really taken the time to get to know the man.

When he'd died, it had just been the passing of a stranger to Morgan. To Leti, it had been the loss of a friend. He wished he'd known about Wyatt then. He wished he knew what to say.

"We can't change the past, Wyatt," Estella said. "The day the Concords attacked the village, Mama and Daddy fought. She was mad because he wanted to go out with his friends that night. They liked to play cards and drink. Mama wanted him to fix the back steps. They died and the last things they said to each other were stupid and spiteful, but I know they loved each other. They knew they loved one another."

117

Wyatt kissed her forehead. "Thank you, sweetie. I know I can't change it."

"It doesn't mean it doesn't hurt though. Daddy didn't say anything to me before he left for work. Mama was grouchy all morning. I failed another math test, and she said that I was too smart to be so lazy. When the attack came, she didn't have time to say anything except *hide*," Estella said. "I think your daddy knew you loved him. That's why he wrote those letters. He couldn't say it himself. I read them with you, Wyatt, and he doesn't say anything about wanting your love. He knew he had it."

Wyatt interlaced his fingers with Morgan's and Estella's, then stared at their joined hands. "You're right. He knew, but he didn't get to hear me say it. Not since I was a kid. I wish I had known then. I wish I could tell him now." He sat up. "If wishes were horses, right? Ugh. My head hurts. I'm sorry for being a big crybaby, guys."

"Mourning your father isn't being a crybaby, Wyatt," Rune said, sitting up and kissing his head. "It's normal, dork." He smoothed down Estella's wild curly hair. "You are one amazing girl."

She stood, head held high. "I am. I'm going to go give Luna a bath and take a shower. I'll go grab us some lunch after that, Wyatt. You need to rest," she said, wagging her finger at him.

After she left, the four of them stared at each other.

"She really is amazing," Wyatt said, "and bossy." He cupped Morgan's face in his hands. "You're amazing too. Thank you for coming. I don't know why, but I always feel better when I'm in your arms."

"I'm out," Rune said, standing and running for the door. Kiki laughed but quickly followed him.

"I feel better when you're in my arms too," Morgan said, placing a kiss on Wyatt's nose. "I would do anything to make you feel better, kitten."

"Anything?"

"Absolutely."

"You would hug Nugget to make me feel better?"

"Okay. Anything but that."

Wyatt laughed, and Morgan couldn't help but smile at the sound. His mate was supposed to laugh and smile, not cry. He couldn't resist kissing Wyatt's smile.

When Wyatt's lips pressed back and he wound his arms around Morgan's neck, Morgan sank into his mate, doing his best to avoid Wyatt's bad leg.

Morgan kissed his way down Wyatt's neck but got distracted by those cute little ears. He nibbled along the lobe of one, then licked the pointed tip.

"Morgan," Wyatt said, moaning and lifting his hips. Morgan couldn't stop himself from rocking against Wyatt, relishing the feel of his mate's hard dick pressing through his pants.

He reached between them and unbuttoned his pants, freeing his erection. He rolled the sweats down Wyatt's hips, then wrapped his fingers around his mate's dick, stroking him. His other hand gripped Wyatt's thigh, spreading him a little wider.

"More," Wyatt said, breathless. "I need more."

Morgan moaned and gripped Wyatt's ear between

his teeth. His grip on Wyatt's thigh tightened, and he pulled his uninjured leg up, their dicks rubbing hard against one another in fast motions. Morgan felt it coming. Everything inside him pulled tight, but he needed something to push him over the edge.

Wyatt spread his legs wide, wrapping his good one around Morgan's hip. Wyatt's smaller body pulled tight, and he screamed as he came, splattering against Morgan's stomach and dick. He shuddered, body undulating, as fierce satisfaction filled his brown eyes.

His mate was far from plain, Morgan thought, coming hard at the sight of Wyatt's satisfaction. He stayed wrapped around Wyatt, enjoying the feeling of rightness. The sun poured through the thick branches of the trees as the ship cruised through the forest, the light glistening off Wyatt's wet skin.

A deep, deep peace filled Morgan, insulating him in gentle warmth. That wasn't sex. That was something so much better.

"Wyatt," Morgan said, giving his mate a gentle kiss. "Thank you."

"Mmm," Wyatt said, looking very sleepy. "We need to clean up."

"You need to sleep. I'll get you clean," Morgan said and ran to the bathroom. He wiped himself down and grabbed a clean rag. He cleaned his beautiful mate, pausing to gently rub his round belly, and pulled Wyatt's pants up. "Get some rest, kitten." He tucked the blankets around his sleepy mate.

"Morgan," Wyatt said, voice soft. The poor man was on the verge of much deserved sleep. "My belly is bigger than it should be at five months. What if I'm having twins? Would that make you run away? We don't *need* to have eight kids. I can compromise."

"I have no idea what you're talking about," Morgan said with a laugh. "If you are having twins, then we'll deal. They're part of you and that makes them my second favorite thing."

"What's your first? You really like your vibro-swords."

"Selene gave them to me," Morgan said. "They aren't my favorite thing though. That would be you. Then the babies and Estella. Then my swords. See? I can compromise too."

Wyatt was laughing as he fell asleep. Morgan watched him for a little while, watched his breaths steady and listened for the soft snore he knew was coming.

"There it is," he whispered when he heard it. He kissed Wyatt's forehead. "I love you, kitten," he said, knowing his mate couldn't hear him. "I love you so damn much."

He made himself move. It was harder than it should have been. He left the room and almost stumbled over Kiki. The redhead sat in the hall next to the door. "You guys finished in there?"

Morgan blushed for the first time in years. "Please tell me you didn't see or hear anything."

"Luckily, I heard a moan when I started in and came right back out. My eyes don't have to be bleached," she said, tapping his ankle with her foot. "There was something I wanted to ask you. Wyatt would just cry all over me."

Morgan sat next to her and waited. Kiki had gotten a lot better, but she was still far too quiet most of the time. She had thoughts swirling around her head, and Morgan figured it took her longer to tame them than it used to.

"I'm never having kids," she said. "Joe and I never really planned to have them, and now, there's no one I would ever want to have them with."

"Never say never, Kiki," Morgan said. "There's no rule that says you won't find another mate one day."

"I don't want another mate," she said roughly. "I wouldn't trade my time with Joe for anything, but I can't do it again. He was my life mate." She shook her head. "Anyway, I'm not having kids. Joe and I were both only children, and there's no family left on either side."

"Wyatt and I are your family now, Kiki. I thought we went over this," he said and wrapped his arm around her shoulders.

"I know you are. That's why I want to give you guys some things." She held out a small key card and two gold rings. "These are our engraved wedding bands. I can't keep carrying them around."

"Kiki, no," he said, thrusting the rings back toward her.

"You'll get around to marrying Wyatt one day. I want you guys to have these. They're full of love and hope, and I can't deal with that now." She wiped her eyes. "The key card is for a storage space. Joe and I had things we couldn't carry with us because they were too big or too valuable. We never wanted to settle anywhere, not even on our breaks, so we bought the storage space. I can't... I can't go there again. We used to check in during every break. We would rent a room nearby and talk about the future, about buying a home one day. I can't go there again, Morgan."

He shook his head violently and tried to hand the card back. "Kiki, when we get off this planet, Wyatt and I will go with you. We'll help you find your closure, okay?"

She ignored him. "There's a bunch of stuff in there. There's a Fire Veil diamond set that was my mom's. My dad bought it a piece at a time, saving for years for each one. She adored it. There's three pieces of vintage Havenite jewelry that's been in Joe's family for generations. There's no one left to give it to. I've made notes on each item stored. I don't want it to end with me. I want you guys to be able to pass it all down to your kids. They aren't just things."

"They're memories," Morgan said in awe. Everything his parents had was stolen when they were murdered. He had nothing from them to hand down to his children except memories and a few photos.

This was too much. Too precious. "Kiki, we can't possibly accept these. You'll find someone again. Your heart will heal, and you'll want it all back."

"No, I won't," she said. She snorted at the look he gave her. "Let's say I do. I can always ask for stuff back. No problem. Please, Morgan. I know we'll leave here soon. I can feel it. I want this settled first. I want you and Wyatt to have those things. They represent our hope and dreams of the future. I need you to carry that on, because I can't."

"Kiki..."

"I know what the future holds for me, and there's no room for hope." Her stubborn look told him he'd have no luck talking her out of this.

"I'll keep them safe for you," he said, giving in. "You will come back for them. I'll get to tell you *I told you so* too."

"Don't hold your breath."

"If you never want them back, I'll let you gift them to our kids, okay? They'll want to hear the stories from their favorite aunt anyway."

She gave him a half smile. "Fine."

"Kiki. It'll get better. It's only been a few months. You'll heal. I know what the future holds for you too, and you won't believe how beautiful it is. Wyatt and I will make damn sure of it."

"How long do you think it'll take you to ask him to marry you?"

"What? Why are we talking about that now? We were having a feelings conversation," Morgan said, surprised at how much he liked the idea of getting hitched to Wyatt. Damn, the difference a few weeks made.

"Don't panic, pretty boy," she said, standing. "It'll happen when it happens. Come on. Alois isn't as mean to the trainees as you are. You need to toughen them up."

14

"Jody has the fleet ready," Dru said, grinning widely. "They have a handy virus for the planetary defense systems and will take them out tomorrow morning. Then they'll be able to get a reading on where the Concords are. We'll strategize from there."

"Finally," Dashel said, whooping. "I can't wait to see those Concords get crushed."

"As long as that creature is alive, the Concords won't be stopped," Kiki said. "Your friends can bomb the whole planet, but that won't kill it. We know now that it can take out cities instantly all by itself. Being in a ship won't be any different than being in a house."

Dru grimaced. "Damn it. You're right."

"What can we do?" Dashel gave them all a determined look. "We'll help any way we can."

"We need to find it," Morgan said. "If we can kill it before Jody attacks, the Concords will be disoriented and vulnerable."

"They'll also be missing their most powerful weapon," Lerais said. "Fuck. If we don't kill it, the best-case scenario is it leaves the planet and goes somewhere else. That just puts others in danger."

"We don't know where it is though," Quinn said. "Wyatt has the poison made, but how do we find the creature before Jody attacks?"

Hazel and Dru exchanged a look. Lerais frowned at his wife. "What do you two know that we don't, sweet mama?"

"When Hazel and I were searching for parts, we overheard good old Uncle Jevio's pilot talking with another man," Dru said.

"The man said the command base was almost ready," Hazel said. "The pilot asked how far it was from where they were at, and the man said it didn't matter, because the city had its own spaceport. They would just fly in there."

"Tammol only has three spaceports," Dashel said. "The closest is in Synegana. The other two are almost a day's drive away, in opposite directions. One to the east and one to the north."

"This needs to be quiet," Kiki said. "Two small teams only. One goes north and one goes east. The only hope we have is to sneak up on the creature. It sees us coming and we're dead."

"Morgan, you take Kiki, Hazel, and two Tammolian volunteers. You go north. I'll take Quinn, Alois, and another two Tammolian volunteers. We have enough of the poison made to give everyone two injectors," Dru said. "Our first priority will be finding him. If the situation allows for it, we kill him. If he can't be taken out through stealth, then retreat. There's no point in wasting lives."

"We'll need to leave as soon as possible," Morgan said. He needed to say goodbye to Wyatt.

"Linc, please stay in contact with Jody as much as possible. She won't be able to call again until they're about to come. Let her know what we're doing and keep us informed of the attack. Lerais, baby, I need you to take charge of our ragtag group here. Protect them."

"You got it, love," he said, cupping her cheek. "You need to be careful though. I won't do well without you."

Half an hour later, after locking Luna in his room, Morgan stood with the others in front of the two shuttles. Wyatt handed each team member two injectors.

"One should do the job, but two would be better," Wyatt said, nervously. "While it looks human, it's not, so this is experimental. Please be careful, guys."

His eyes met Morgan's, and he couldn't stand the fear he saw.

Morgan strode forward, pulling Wyatt into his arms. He was half aware of Dashel saying goodbye to Rasha and the kids, Narin hugging Mayla, and Dru kissing Lerais. "Kitten, it'll be okay."

"You don't know that. You didn't see that thing in action. This is going to be next to impossible. I've only just found you, Morgan. I don't want to lose you."

"I'll do my best to make sure you don't lose me," Morgan said. "I can't promise to never die, but I want to live. I want to come back to you. I won't take unnecessary risks." He stroked Wyatt's cheeks and wiped the tears away. Someone caught his eyes. Two someones. "Wait, what are they doing?"

Pela and Rune walked up, medic bags on their shoulders. "We're volunteering," Pela said. "Each team gets a medic to wait in the shuttle. That way, you won't have to go hours with no help if someone's injured."

"You know it's dangerous, right? We can't promise your safety," Dru said.

"We know," Rune said. "It's our decision."

"Thank you," Dru said, nodding to each of them. "I won't say no to onsite medics."

Morgan watched Wyatt hug Kiki and Rune as Pela climbed into his shuttle. Thin, strong arms wrapped around his middle, and he looked down into Estella's worried eyes.

"You have to come back, Morgan," she said. "I'll take care of Wyatt and Luna while you're gone, but we all need you. Okay?"

He picked the girl up and spun her around, hugging her tightly. He treasured her giggles. "I will do my best, sweetie. I love you too, you know."

"I love you," she said. "Wyatt and I both do. He'll tell you when you get back."

"Now I really have to come back," he said, laughing.

"That's life," she said, shrugging.

He kissed Wyatt one more time, then forced himself to get into the shuttle. Their city was nine hours away, so they needed to get going.

He turned around, looking at everyone. "You all

sure about going? It's okay if you'd rather not. This mission is going to be sketchy as hell."

Each person met his eyes with no hesitancy.

"We're ready," Narin said.

"We all know the risks, Morgan," Dashel said.

He looked at Pela. "All of us," she said.

"Let's get moving," Morgan said, turning back around. His damn ulcer was back.

"THIS CITY IS A LOT LARGER," Hazel said. "There's a lot more activity too."

Morgan parked the shuttle behind a pile of crashed vehicles near the spaceport. This city looked a lot like the other one, only bigger and busier.

"This is the capital of Tammol," Dashel said. "I visited once when I was a teenager. The President of the Commonwealth was stationed in the largest blue government building, right in the center of town. What do you want to bet that's where they're focused?"

"How the hell are we going to get in there?" Narin watched the heavy traffic above them.

"First, here are your ear communicators. They link only to each other." Morgan handed them out and everyone turned them on. "Next, take extra shields. I have a feeling we'll have to fight our way out. If you get stranded and can't get back to the shuttle before we leave, make your way to the farm we passed next to the river to the east. We'll have a shuttle there in the morning."

"We should scout a bit first," Kiki said. "See how much of the city they've occupied. We also might be able to pick up some uniforms. That will help us sneak in."

"You, Pela, and Morgan, maybe," Hazel said. "The rest of us are too non-human to blend."

"True," Kiki said. She turned to Morgan. "I'll go in first and look around."

"Be careful," he said. "Take your armor off. If you're scouting, plan on blending."

Kiki left and they waited. Morgan hated it. He was usually the one at the front, not the one waiting in the shuttle. Fuck. This sucked. An hour later, Kiki came back with a bag of clothes and armor.

"Good news is there are plenty of Concords fully armored, so Hazel, Dashel, and Narin can wear full armor to cover up. Bad news is there are plenty of fucking Concords. The city is a fully functional Concord hold now."

"Okay. Here's the plan. Three teams go in and head separately toward the government buildings. We stay in contact and see what we see. Hazel, take Dashel and Narin with you. The three of you will match and can look like you're on duty. Kiki and I will both go on our own. Hustle. No matter what. Pela, if we aren't here in three hours, fly to the farm."

"Okay," she said.

Morgan entered the city separately from the others, walking at a fast pace, as if he had somewhere important to be. He carried his vibro-swords and phaser in a bag. Kiki was right. This was definitely a Concord city now.

He grabbed a ride on a shuttle-tram and watched the large white and blue buildings get closer. The tram stopped several times, letting Concords off and on as it drew closer to the center of town. Two men got on the tram together and sat near Morgan.

"I get feeding duty today," one said.

The other man shivered. "I fed it yesterday. That thing is so fucking creepy. I have to keep reminding myself that it's on our side."

"At least we have plenty of uglies to feed it," the first man said, laughing.

When they got ready to exit, Morgan followed them, sticking close to the man with feeding duty. He must have been talking about the creature. Keeping his head down and whispering, he filled the others in on what he'd overheard. "I'm following him now."

"Yes," Hazel said. "We needed some luck."

"What do you think he's feeding the creature?" Narin asked.

"Tammolians," Kiki answered bluntly. "I didn't think they were keeping prisoners, but what else could it be?"

"We can't leave them here," Dashel said.

"No, we can't," Morgan agreed. "Start heading my way. I'll let you know the plan as soon as I see what's going on."

The man he followed entered a small, white building. It was only four down from the largest blue building that Dashel had mentioned. No guards were outside the building, but there were several within it. They milled around, checking IDs at each door.

Morgan saw the man go down a flight of stairs. The guards avoided even looking at that exit. Strange. He followed him, ducking under the stairs when he saw the man stopped at a locked door.

The man pressed his hand to the scanner and it opened. Morgan managed to grab the door before it closed behind him, but just barely. He waited a moment, then eased the door open and slipped in. He left the door cracked behind him.

It was another large room like the one above, but without the windows. Morgan barely saw the man disappearing down another flight of steps. He casually followed behind. All in all, they descended six stories into the ground. Morgan left each door cracked.

"Found your open door," Hazel said. "We're coming behind you."

The last door was guarded, and the man stopped to talk. Morgan settled his bag on the ground behind the stairs.

"You lucked out today, huh?"

"Yeah. I have to feed it."

"We have lots of uglies to choose from."

Morgan pulled his phaser out and fired three quick shots. None of them were wearing shields. "Idiots."

He dragged two of the dead men behind the stairs and grabbed his bag. Using the remaining man's hand, he opened the door and peeked in. It looked like an empty break room. He stuck his bag in front of the door and dragged the third body away. He shut the door behind him and slung his bag over his shoulder. "Okay, guys. I'm somewhere. Don't know where."

"Wow. That is so helpful," Hazel said.

"Shut it," he said, growling. He ignored her laughter and looked around. It was really quiet down here. There was a bathroom to the right and a set of double doors straight ahead. "Dashel, any idea what this building is?"

"No idea," Dashel said. "The prison is all the way across the city, so I don't know what this is supposed to be."

The three walked in behind him. "What's the plan?" Hazel asked.

"I guess we see what's through those doors," Morgan said. He pushed through the double doors and walked down the long hallway. The only door he could see was the one at the end. "We may need to go grab that guy I was following."

"On it," Dashel said, spinning around and running back the way they'd come.

"Yep. The door's locked," Hazel said. She pressed her ear against it. "I hear people back there. It's crying and stuff, so probably the prisoners."

"How are we going to get them out of here?" Narin asked.

"One thing at a time," Morgan said. Dashel came back with the man thrown over his shoulder. Morgan used the man's hand to open the door before walking through. He heard the thump as Dashel left the man's body behind. Hundreds of cells lined the walls of the large room. They were full to bursting with Tammolians. "Fuck."

"What are you doing here?" A fully armored Concord guard got out of his chair. "Is it dinner time? They don't usually send this many to get one."

"It's my first time doing this, so I asked some buddies to come with," Morgan said pleasantly. "To be honest, I don't even know where to take the meal."

The guard laughed. "Did you lose a bet? You did, didn't you?"

Morgan grinned sheepishly. "Maybe."

"The Admiral's pet is in the biggest blue building in the government square, four buildings over from this one. Have you been there?"

"Not even once."

"Well, its room is on the top floor. Just look for the place everyone's avoiding. As long as you have an ugly with you, no one will bother you."

"I just lead the meal through the streets? Will that be okay?"

"Oh yeah," the guard said. "It's a daily routine now. Everyone's used to it."

"What happens when we run out of meals?" Morgan asked, nodding toward the hundreds of Tammolians.

"There's pockets of Tammolians hidden all over the planet," the man said, laughing. "They think they got away, can you believe it? We fuck with them all the time. When we run out here, we'll go round a couple of the hidden groups up. These uglies are so fucking stupid."

"Wow," Morgan said, not having to fake his surprise. "I didn't know. Any other tips?"

"Make sure you bring the body to the nearest trash compactor. The Admiral doesn't like to see them lying around his pet's rooms. So, do you want a man, woman, or child? We got them all," the guard said.

"Can I?" Dashel asked.

"Go for it." Morgan nodded.

The guard was dead in seconds, a hole in his forehead from Dashel's phaser.

Morgan looked around the large room full of people. "How the hell are we going to get them all out? There's thousands here."

"You're here to help us?" An old Tammolian man pressed against the bars closest to them.

"Yes. We just need to figure out how to do that," Morgan said.

"There are access tunnels," the man said. "Under the city. There's a door to one three floors up."

"How do you know that?" Narin asked, removing his helmet.

"I was a janitor for this place. It was a Commonwealth science lab. I know where the tunnels are, but I don't know where they come out at. I've never been in them. They were used to maintain public transit, a couple hundred years ago, so there's no telling what kind of shape they're in," the man said.

"Okay. That's better than trying to walk you all out through the streets. Pela, stay ready to move the shuttle if we need you to." There was no response, just silence. "Pela?"

15

"I'm sorry, Morgan," Pela said. "Kiki needed my help. I put on one of the uniforms and snuck in."

"What happened? Kiki?"

"Someone recognized me from the village. We're holed up in a bathroom with a dead body. My leg and arm wouldn't stop bleeding."

"I got it stopped, but she's really weak," Pela said. "She can walk, but she'll need our help to make it all the way out of the city."

"Where are you? I'll come get you." Morgan gestured to the guard's keys, and Hazel and Narin started unlocking the cells.

"That building Dashel was talking about," Kiki said.

"That's the building where the creature is," Morgan said.

"We were listening while I got Kiki stabilized. We heard what that man said." Pela's voice was strained. "Kiki and I have an idea, but you're not going to like it."

"Fuck," Morgan said. "What's your plan?"

"We escort his meal to him," Pela said. "I can pull my hair back and take my contacts out. It's not as noticeable as the Tammolians, but I'm not human."

"I don't like it."

"Told you that you wouldn't," Pela said. "The creature needs to be stopped, Morgan. Do you have a better plan? This will at least get us close to it."

"You need a Tammolian," Dashel said, shaking his head. "You could use Pela, but it'll be more convincing with an *ugly*." He helped the elderly man sit in the guard's seat. "Will you switch clothes with me?"

"I'm more your size," another man said. "Rally's pants would be shorts on you."

"Thank you," Dashel said, and the men undressed.

"Kiki, Pela, we're on our way, alright?"

"Okay," Pela said. "We'll rest up while we wait."

"Hazel, you and Narin get these people into the tunnels. Try to find an exit, but stay hidden until you hear from us," Morgan said.

"Yes, sir," Hazel said, nodding. She turned to the growing crowd. "Anyone who can't walk gets carried. Be as quiet as possible but move fast. Let's go." They all rushed up the stairs, Rally and Hazel leading the group of Tammolians behind them, while Narin brought up the rear.

"Here it is," Rally said. Morgan and Dashel had to work together to get the old hatch open. It was only about two foot high.

Hazel started helping people through. "We got this, sir," she said. "Good luck."

"Thanks, Hazel. Be careful. If you get a chance, call Dru and let her know what's happening," Morgan said.

He led Dashel up the rest of the stairs and out of the building. The streets were busier than before, but the crowds kept far away from the two of them.

The Concords did their best not to look at Dashel. The guard had been right. Everyone expected this. They knew what would be done to the *ugly*.

He entered the central building and easily made his way past guards and other Concord officials. He saw Ralen Jevio's uncle on the third floor, speaking with a familiar-looking man. He made it to the restroom Pela and Kiki were hiding in.

"We're here," he said.

The two women marched out, Kiki paler than he'd ever seen her. Sweat covered her forehead and he could tell she was in pain.

"Are you going to be alright?" he asked, smoothing her hair from her face.

"I have to be," Kiki said.

Pela wore one of the sets of armor, her face hidden behind a helmet and her medic bag slung over her shoulder. Her hands shook.

"Pela, you don't have to go. You and Kiki can both wait right here," Morgan said.

"No," Pela said. "I'm scared, but I *will* see that thing dead."

"I won't stay back," Kiki said. "Deal with it."

"Stubborn women," Dashel said, hiding a smile.

"Let's get to the top floor," Morgan said. The three of them walked through five more floors of

Concords. Like on the street, the men and women around them did their best to avoid looking their way.

As attacks went, this was by far the easiest he'd ever led. They'd found Tammolians and had an easy way to rescue them. They'd located the creature and had an easy way to get to him. Except for Kiki's scuffle, luck was on their side.

The hallways of the top two floors were deserted. "No one wants to be near him, do they?" Dashel looked up and down the empty hall.

"I don't blame them," Pela said, removing her helmet. Her hair was pulled up, revealing her pointed ears. "He's one floor up, and I swear I can feel him."

"I promise it's that fucking redhead I told you about." The voice came from the stairwell and was followed by the sound of several footsteps.

"Pela, Plan B," Kiki said, grabbing Dashel's arm.

Pela grabbed him and something jabbed his arm. His body went lax. Pela lowered him to the floor. "I'm sorry, Morgan. It's just a sedative, and you'll wake up in about fifteen minutes." She kissed his head. "Plan B was my idea. I don't want to die, but you have babies on the way, and Dashel has a family. Tell my dads and my little sister that I loved them. Tell them I chose this. I'm a Charybdis soldier."

His vision started to dim, and he barely saw Dashel's body settle beside his.

"Tell Wyatt and Rune I love them," Kiki said softly. "I'm ready to be with Joe again."

He heard the Concords rush the hall. "There she is.

That bitch must be helping her. They killed the other guard and the ugly," one of them said.

"Let's show them the penthouse. They seem so eager to get there." Laughter filled his ears as everything faded to black.

MORGAN WOKE WITH A START, sitting up straight. "Kiki. Pela."

Dashel moaned, sitting up. "What the fuck?"

"Kiki said Plan B. What the hell was Plan B?" Morgan struggled to his feet, shaking off the lethargy. He helped Dashel to his feet.

"There were over twenty of them," Dashel said. "It was the last thing I saw after Kiki drugged me."

"We could have taken them," Morgan said, growling. He pulled his phasers from his bag and strapped them on. He grabbed his swords and the harness next. After activating his shield, he started toward the last flight of stairs.

"Not without alerting the creature," Dashel said, pulling his own weapons and shield from Morgan's bag. "Then we'd all die. What did they do? They can't have gotten close enough to it as prisoners."

They walked up the steps and were greeted by bright sunshine. The top floor was all windows overlooking the city. It looked like a penthouse apartment, lavish and well decorated. The circle of Concord mercenaries standing by a blood smeared window stood out.

"What are we going to do?" one of them asked. "The Admiral will kill us all. He'll give us to the other one."

"How did they kill it? He didn't even touch them. How did they kill it?" The man ran his hands through his hair, desperation making him shake. "He just shook and fucking exploded."

Morgan saw their bodies in the middle of the living room. Kiki and Pela held hands, their wasted bodies face down.

"They stuck themselves," Morgan whispered harshly, eyes filling with tears. The injectors were still in their thighs. They had poisoned themselves right before the creature drained them.

"Stubborn women," Dashel said, voice thick and tears falling down his cheeks.

"They didn't kill you?" One of the Concords faced them, and the others slowly turned to them. "The bitches killed the Admiral's pet."

"Their names were Kiki and Pela, and they were Charybdis soldiers," Morgan said. "You should know that before you die."

He drew his blades.

Dashel ducked behind a couch, pulling his phasers out and firing the first shots. He hit three square in the chest before the group moved.

The idiots were slow to activate their shields and bumbled around for precious seconds.

Dashel killed four more of them. The man could fucking shoot.

Morgan cleared his mind, finding the quiet place Selene had shown him. Everything slowed down, and he moved, vibro-swords swirling, cutting easily through the Concord mercs' shields.

He wanted to see them bleed.

It didn't take long. Twenty-six to two weren't good odds, but it still didn't take long. The last Concord merc knelt on the floor in front of him.

"Please," the merc said. "Mercy. Please."

Tell my dads and my little sister that I loved them. Tell them I chose this. I'm a Charybdis soldier. I'm ready to be with Joe again.

Morgan shook his head and brought his blade down. The man's head rolled across the floor.

Dashel stepped around the pile of bodies surrounding Morgan. "Morgan, I didn't know anyone could move like that. I thought we were dead. There were twenty-six of them. Fuck." He ran his hands through his hair.

Together they turned to look at the creature's body... Well, the pieces of mush covering a chair by the window.

"Does this resemble the creature that attacked your village?" Morgan asked Dashel.

"It seemed a little less squishy to be honest." Dashel frowned, then knelt on the floor, poking around under the chair. "Eww. This is disgusting."

"Let's get out of here," Morgan said. "Put on one of the more intact armored uniforms. We'll... We'll carry them out."

MORGAN FLEW the stolen personal shuttle out of the city. Kiki and Pela's bodies were in the back. Morgan would make damn sure Kiki was placed with her husband and Pela's remains made it to her dads.

Dashel sat in silence, thoughts obviously heavy. "Right before she drugged me, Kiki said that it was always going to be this way. She said I had a family to worry about, so she'd fight for me. For Tammol."

"The two of them made more than one plan while they were stuck in the bathroom," Morgan said. He felt numb. He'd seen death. He'd lost friends before. It felt different this time. Maybe it was because of Pela. She had been so young. Maybe it was because of Kiki. Maybe it was because he knew this would hurt Wyatt.

His stomach cramped. Damn responsibility. Damn Concords.

"They killed it though," Dashel said. "They stopped that thing from hurting anyone else."

"They did. Those stubborn, brave idiots killed it." His voice broke, and he took a deep breath. They weren't done yet. They got out of the car and moved the bodies to the shuttle.

He settled into the driver's seat. "Hazel, can you hear me?"

"Yes, sir," she said. "I didn't want to distract you all. How's it going?"

"The creature is dead," Morgan said.

"Yes!" she said, cheering. "Wait, you sound sad. What's wrong?"

"Kiki and Pela didn't make it out. They killed the creature, but died doing it."

"Oh," she said, squeaking. "Oh, no."

"What about you all? Are you making any progress?"

"Rally knows his city," Narin said. "We're heading toward the east. He thinks there's an exit there. It might be near that farm you mentioned."

"We'll go there and wait for you," Morgan said.

"I called Dru during a break," Hazel said. Her rough voice told him she had been crying. "I updated her. Her team got in a scuffle at their assigned city and didn't get very far inside. Captain was badly injured, but Rune saved her. She's not great, but she's not dead." Her voice went high at the end. She cleared her throat. "Quinn got shot too, but she's okay. They'll be okay."

"Good," he said. "I'll give her a call while we wait for you. Stay in contact."

"Yes, sir."

16

"*J*'m sorry, Wyatt. I couldn't keep them safe," Morgan said, his voice deep and uneven. Wyatt didn't think it was because of the communicator. He wished he could see his mate's face, that he could touch and hold him, but the connection wasn't good enough.

"I think Kiki stopped wanting to live the second she felt Joe die," Wyatt said softly. "She stayed alive to protect us. Fuck, she basically handed over her last will and testament." He had to cover his mouth to muffle the sob. He had to keep it together. "Morgan, she was a grown woman, and I know she made the choice she did to keep you and Dashel alive."

"It's what I would have done. Before I met you, if Hack had been in danger, I would have given my life for him. He had a mate and a bunch of damn kids. I wouldn't have hesitated. It's different, being on this side of it," Morgan said. "Pela was so damn young, Wyatt."

Wyatt couldn't stop his whimper this time. "I know. She was something special. It doesn't surprise me, not really. We spent a lot of time talking about the poison and the different ways to get it into the creature."

"Fuck me," Morgan said. "This sucks so much. Everything went too smoothly, too easily at first. I should have known." He was quiet for a minute. "Have you heard from Jody?"

"Lerais and I spoke with her. She's going to call again in three hours to get an update. I'll tell her about the creature and the main hub. We'll get a ship to you to pick up all the people you rescued before the full attack begins."

"Good," he said. "Thank you for listening, kitten. Thank you for not hating me."

"I could never hate you, baby," Wyatt said, shaking his head. His mate took too much on his shoulders. He had to learn to balance it all or he'd have a permanent upset tummy. "Kiki and Pela saved us. They saved you and Dashel. They saved this planet and all the planets that thing would have destroyed. That was their decision, and it was a beautiful, heart-breaking choice, but it was *their* choice. Not yours."

"I love you, Wyatt," Morgan said. "I love your heart, your dorkiness, your smile, that big brain, your plump ass. I love you so damn much."

"Morgan," Wyatt said, mortified and happy at the same time. "Estella's listening."

The little girl smacked his butt and laughed. "He loves your butt, Wyatt."

"I do," Morgan agreed. "I love everything about him, Estella."

"I love you too," Wyatt said, blushing.

"What do you love about him?" Estella poked his side and gave him a look. "You gotta say."

"Hmm," Wyatt said. "I love his confidence and his mama mentality with his crew. I love that he's a dork too, so we work together. He would so dance with me for the patients. I love that he takes responsibility. He steps up when he has to, even though it's hard and painful. Oh, and he may love my butt, but I love his muscles. He has so many yummy, yummy muscles. Have you *seen* his shoulders, Estella?"

"Eww," Estella said. "You two are so gross."

"We're gross and in love," Morgan said. Wyatt could hear his smile. "I'll be with you two soon."

"Three," Wyatt said. "Don't forget Luna."

"Of course. I meant I'll be with you three soon."

"Talk to Dru," Wyatt said. "She's really upset that she missed all the action. She feels like she traumatized you since you had to deal with everything."

"Oh, fuck. She's going to want to have another *feelings* talk. I hate those."

"It's her awkward, caring captain thing. Deal with it."

The call ended, and Wyatt hugged Estella, trying not to cry. He needed to be strong, but Kiki and Pela weren't coming home. Estella laid her head on his shoulder.

"Remember right after they attacked the village,"

she said. "I cried and cried and cried. We all did. It's okay to cry. Our friends are dead."

She buried her face in his neck, and they cried together.

"KIKI AND PELA ARE DEAD. Rune is bringing us a heavily injured team. Both of your mates are out there with over a thousand rescued Tammolians, and to top it all off, a fleet is about to attack the planet. You really want to do this now?" Jane watched them in disbelief, then threw her hands in the air when Wyatt and Rasha just looked at her.

He leaned back and handed her the scanner.

Rasha sat behind him, cuddling against his back. "This is the perfect time to do this," the Tammolian woman said. "Death and worry are everywhere. Let's have a little joy while we wait for the next act to start."

"My god, you are too wise and shit when you're not slowly dying and in pain," Jane said and growled. "Fine."

She scanned his belly, recording as much as possible then handed it back to him. "What's in there, Doc?"

Several moments passed as he looked through the images and read the recorded information. "My cholesterol is a little high," he said finally.

"Wyatt Morrick!" Jane smacked his arm. "Tell us how many babies are in there, damn it!"

"Two," he said slowly, feeling it sink into his heart. "Two girls."

"Kiki and Pela Morrick," Estella said. "That's their names, right?"

"You're damn right, that's their names," Jane said, wiping her eyes. "Those two... Those two won't be forgotten. Neither will Joe, Lolani, and Ron. We'll make sure of it."

Rasha kissed the side of his head. "Jody will be calling in about ten minutes. Let's get to the conference room. Estella, you will watch my two babies, won't you?"

"Of course," the little girl said, rolling her eyes. "I already have games planned. I'll keep them busy. You two gotta help save the planet, and Jane needs to watch the med-bay."

"You're a sweet girl," Wyatt said. "You're also sassy. Mind your manners, little miss." He poked her shoulder.

She blushed. "I roll my eyes too much, right?"

"We know where you learned it," Jane said, eyes on Wyatt.

He rolled his eyes. They were all ridiculous. "Come on, Rasha. Let's do this thing."

Lerais and Linc were already there. The conference room was so empty with both teams still away. Dru and her group were coming home, but it was a long flight. As soon as Wyatt's butt touched the chair, Jody's call came through.

Her face popped up on the screen and Wyatt smiled. He couldn't help it. She was a happy, confident, beautiful woman, and she was smiling at him.

"You all ready for a rescue? The Foxtail Coalition is

on its way, baby brother. I have volunteers from six other mercenary bands and some extras I think you'll like."

"Hell yes," Lerais exclaimed. "The ship is as good as it's going to get until I can get more parts, and I know the Tammolians are eager to get their planet back."

"What about that murder monster you all mentioned?"

"It's dead," Wyatt said. "There is a large group of Tammolians who need your help right away too."

He quickly updated her on Morgan's mission.

"I'll get a ship down there first thing. We got a couple of folks from the Half-Moon Guild that are helping out. Their ships are basically invisible. We'll send them to Morgan. Any suggestions on where to hit first? We'll do a scan for population, but we'll have more of an advantage earlier on. We need to be quick."

"I would suggest taking out the two largest spaceports," Rasha said. "If you can, try to leave the one in Synegana intact. It would be best to hit the capital first, I think, but that is where Morgan and the rescued Tammolians are."

"Half-Moon works fast. They'll be out of there within the first hour of the attack. We'll focus on the other spaceport first, then hit the capital. Shit. I got to go. If I stay still too long, the defenses could detect me. I'll call in once the defenses are down."

"Bye, Jody," Lerais said and the call ended.

"I can't believe this is happening," Rasha said.

"We'll get your planet back, Rasha," Linc said. "Start planning what you'll do with it." He looked to Lerais.

"Should we start toward Dru since Morgan won't be flying back anytime soon?"

"Good idea. Things are about to get chaotic, so it'd be best if she was with us. Get everyone loaded up and we'll set out," Lerais said. "Rasha, you need to let them know what's happening."

"I'll tell them," she said, nodding.

Dashel and Rasha had become the Tammolian group's unofficial leaders in the past few weeks. Rasha had a way of keeping them calm and focused. Wyatt stayed where he was, waiting for Jody's next call. He might not be a fighter, but he would help any way he could.

WYATT RAN DOWN THE HALL, darting between people with Estella and Luna at his heels. He carried one of Rasha's kids on his back, and the little boy squealed with joy as he passed people in the hall. Rasha ran beside him, carrying her oldest.

The attack had begun and within the first six hours, Jody's Foxtail Coalition had retaken Synegana and destroyed one of the other two spaceports.

A day later, the surprise was gone and the Concords were ready for them. The fight had really begun. They were in the process of attacking the capital now, but Wyatt didn't care. All he cared about was his mate.

They reached the shuttle as the two men were getting out. Rasha and Dashel's little boy slid down Wyatt's back and went running to his papa. Wyatt threw himself into his mate's arms, burrowing his face into Morgan's neck. He made room for Estella, and the two hugged Morgan close while Luna ran around them in circles.

"I'm back, kitten. I'm here," Morgan said, kissing his cheek. "Are you guys okay?"

"We're fine," Estella said, head buried against Wyatt's belly. "You're back, so we're fine."

"Estella, will you come with us to the commons. We're hungry," Hazel said. She had a hold of Rasha's two boys. Narin and Mayla stood with her, waiting for Wyatt's girl.

"Are you guys going to kiss and stuff while I'm gone?" Estella eyed Morgan and Wyatt.

"Yes," Wyatt said. "We're going to kiss the whole damn time you're gone."

"Fine. I'm taking Luna with me. She doesn't need to see that," Estella said, calling the dog to her. "I'll bring you both dinner in a few hours."

"Lock the door," Rasha said with a smirk.

"Don't smirk at me," Wyatt said. "Where are you two going?"

"To Hazel's room. To kiss," she answered.

Hazel gagged. "Come on, everyone. I want to keep my appetite."

"Hug me first," Wyatt said. He hugged Hazel and Narin, then pulled Dashel into his arms while Rasha fussed over Morgan.

"I found this, Wyatt," Dashel said, handing him a small pyramid shaped box. "The creature wore it around his neck, remember? It was the only way I could recognize its remains. I thought you might want it."

"Thank you, Dashel. I'll look into it a bit. See if it can tell us anything about the monster." Wyatt stuck it in the large pocket of his lab coat right before Morgan pulled him out of Dashel's arms.

"In a hurry?" he asked his mate, laughing at Morgan's growl.

Morgan pulled Wyatt behind him, moving quickly through the halls. He locked the door as soon as they were in their room and spun around, pressing Wyatt against the wall. Their lips met, and Wyatt lost it. He crawled up Morgan's body, wrapping his legs around his waist and grinding against him. His mate was finally home.

They slid down the wall, ending up on the floor, and Morgan easily picked Wyatt up and arranged him until he straddled his lap. Wyatt felt the hard erection pressing against him and moaned. He couldn't help but push hungrily against the large bulge. His mate felt so good against him.

Morgan gripped Wyatt's ass in one of his hands and pulled him down, rubbing against him. He cupped the back of Wyatt's neck and turned his face toward him. Morgan's golden-brown eyes glowed with heat, and his hungry expression softened.

"I love you so much, Wyatt. I wasn't going to do this yet, but you make it impossible not to." His voice was uneven and gruff.

Morgan's took his mouth again, and Wyatt couldn't think, only feel. The hand on the back of his neck held him still so Morgan could explore his mouth. His mate's tongue wrapped around his, and Wyatt couldn't help but move his hips again. His mate tasted so fucking good. As their mouths moved together, Morgan fought to pull Wyatt's pants down his legs.

Wyatt ran his hands down Morgan's chest, moaning in frustration. He wanted skin, damn it. His fingers reached the front of Morgan's pants, and he managed to unfasten them as Morgan stroked his dick. Wyatt pulled his lips away from Morgan's and leaned his hips back. He looked down between them, freeing Morgan's long, thick cock. His hole clenched at the thought of the thick shaft inside him. He stroked Morgan once, then used his thumb to rub at the pearl of pre-cum that leaked from the tip.

Morgan's strokes increased, distracting him. He whimpered, then reached behind himself, tracing his hole. "Morgan, I want you in me." He carefully stretched himself. "I need lube."

Morgan buried his face against his neck. "Anything for you." He jumped up and ran to their bags, shucking his boots and pants. In seconds, he was back beneath Wyatt, his fingers buried in his hole.

"Fuck. You're so tight," Morgan said, groaning. He lifted Wyatt until he was poised above Morgan's aching cock. "You love me. Say it, kitten," he ordered roughly.

"I love you so much, Morgan. I need you in me now. Right fucking now."

Morgan shuddered beneath him, then pulled his mate's hips down, impaling Wyatt on his dick. He pushed until he was completely inside, then brought

Wyatt's mouth back to his. Morgan kissed him deeply, his hand guiding Wyatt's hips, establishing a rhythm.

Wyatt rode him hard, hands braced on his shoulders, and it wasn't long before he came, soaking Morgan's stomach and chest with his release.

Morgan growled, then moved faster against him. He pressed his mouth against Wyatt's shoulder. As he pumped deep inside him, he buried his teeth in Wyatt's body. Wyatt screamed as hot pleasure poured through him and he came again. His ass clenched around Morgan who cried out as he came, filling Wyatt.

When he finished shuddering, Morgan pulled Wyatt close and kissed the top of his head. They smelled of sex and home.

"Wipe that smug look off your face," Wyatt said breathlessly.

"Why should I? That was so damn good."

"You bit me!"

"Uh-huh," Morgan said, unconcerned.

"I feel branded. You branded me!"

Morgan licked his bite mark. "So I did."

Wyatt sighed, giving up his outrage. He wiggled, settling into his mate's arms. "I love you, mate."

"Love you more."

17

THREE MONTHS LATER

*W*yatt sat between Morgan and Estella in the largest courtyard in the center of Synegana, Tammol's new capital. His friends sat in the seats around him. He propped his hands on his big belly and watched Rasha and Dashel walk slowly to the edge of the balcony overlooking the courtyard.

The surviving Tammolians cheered loudly as the couple looked out at the crowd.

"Today, is the first day for a new Tammol," Rasha said, voice full of surety and confidence. "Thanks to our friends in the Foxtail Coalition, the last of the Concords have been chased from our world."

The crowd cheered, and Wyatt joined in, shouting loudly.

"Through the sacrifice of two wonderful, brave women, the Concords' creature, the monster that murdered millions of our people, is dead," Rasha said. The crowd roared, standing and stomping. Estella bounced beside Wyatt as they all cheered with the Tammolians. "Our planet again belongs to us!"

Dashel stepped forward. "This is a day we will always remember and will always celebrate, but there is work to be done." Wyatt looked around. The crowd watched the couple, utterly focused on their newly elected leaders. "You elected my wife and me, two country villagers, to lead you to a new future, and that is what we intend to do. There is no Commonwealth. There is no Resistance. There is only Tammol."

The crowds were on their feet again, and Wyatt had to wipe his eyes. These people had been at war with each other for over twenty years.

"The first problem we face is our greatest," Rasha said. "Look around you. This is all that is left of our people. Where once we were a small planet of almost fifty-two million people, we are now a ravaged planet of exactly one million, seven hundred, and thirty-two people. Think about that. Think of what we have lost."

"We've spoken with the Council that you elected to help us lead you," Dashel said. "We've thought and thought on how to protect ourselves now that we are vulnerable. We've listened to your suggestions. We've consulted with our off-world friends. Finally, we have made a decision. It's one many of you whole-heartedly support."

Jody stepped out on the balcony, joining Rasha and Dashel. The crowd cheered loudly, knowing what was coming.

"With your support," Rasha said. "We asked our

dear friend to consider joining us, to consider becoming Tammolian." Wyatt watched Jody blush. The woman was crazy and fierce. She reminded him so much of Kiki before Joe died. "Jody and her Foxtail Coalition, every last one of them, have agreed to become ours. They are bringing their families and friends with them."

Wyatt and the crowd stood again, roaring their approval.

Dashel laughed. "We are also accepting refuges from other planets and systems. They need homes, and we need more people. I hope this will make Tammol a diverse, evolving world. One that can protect itself from any who want to take it."

He looked at the crowd. "Today is a day of celebration. It's a day of freedom and of rebirth, but also a day of remembrance. Remember those we lost, our families and our friends. The Foxtail soldiers that died fighting for us. Our beloved Kiki and Pela, the women who killed the Concords' creature. We must not forget."

The three turned away and disappeared back into the building. "I can't believe Jody is moving here," Dru said from behind them. She rose gingerly from her chair. "I thought she said she'd never live anywhere but her ship."

"Her crew started wanting a home. They've been together a long time. All those people who volunteered from the other mercenary groups want the same thing," Lerais said, arm holding his wife steady. "I think that's why they volunteered. They understood what the Tammolians lost."

"Well, they'll definitely be protected from any vultures," Morgan said. "That woman knows how to run a team."

"It'll also give all these refugees we keep finding on Concord ships somewhere to go besides Charybdis Station," Alois said. The Dedril looked handsome in his official Charybdis uniform. He still limped from his own injuries. The war had been short, but hard on everyone. "Dashel said they weren't going to refuse any species."

"Jane and Garen are staying too," Wyatt said, glaring at his friend. She just shrugged and stuck her tongue out at him. He was sad that he wouldn't see Jane every day, but he knew she was more than done with the GACP. She and Garen both loved Tammol. They'd fought for it alongside the Foxtails.

"I know you two will be welcomed," Lerais said. "Garen, you're a cooking god. If I was gay and wasn't in love with Dru, I'd steal you from Jane."

"Fuck. We can have a triad marriage," Dru said. "Bring him on."

"You can't have my husband," Jane said, laughing. "Quit trying to steal him."

"You won't leave us, will you, Rune?" Wyatt gave his friend his best puppy eyes.

"Nope. I'll go where you do, Doc. I'm your nurse. Well, unless something better comes along," Rune said.

"I feel so loved," Wyatt said, poking the big lug in the shoulder.

"Now that the Concords are gone and the planet will be protected, we can leave," Morgan said, looking at Wyatt. "You know your mom is waiting for us on Rueal. She doesn't know you're about to pop out twins either."

"Don't remind me," Wyatt said. "At least I told her about Estella. She'll just find out she'll have three granddaughters instead of just one."

Morgan laughed and helped him walk back toward their rooms in the new presidential building. Estella grabbed Wyatt's free hand, swinging it back and forth. She still insisted on becoming a doctor and living with Wyatt.

To be honest, he was relieved. He'd grown so attached to the little girl and loved her.

"I'm going to call Sebastian, then take a nap," Wyatt said. "When are we leaving?"

"Tomorrow morning," Dru said.

Alois danced him away from Morgan. "I told you that you and my Sebastian would be best friends, didn't I?"

"You did," Wyatt said. "You didn't mention Leti and Shae though, so it doesn't count."

"Give me back my mate," Morgan said. He looked all growly and fierce, at least until Linc walked by, Nugget stretched across his shoulders. "Back, demon cat. Back." Nugget just looked at him and gave a half-hearted hiss.

"Lazy thing," Linc said, scratching her head. "You could at least attack him when he calls you demon cat."

"Linc," Morgan said. "How could you say such a thing?"

Wyatt pulled Morgan and Estella into their rooms. "I'll save you, baby. Don't worry about that fierce demon cat." He shut the door to his friends' laughter. Estella yawned. "Why don't you lie down for a bit, sweetie? We're going to have to say our goodbyes tonight, and you won't want to be half-asleep."

"Okay," she said, yawning again. She went to her room.

He looked at Morgan, shaking his head. The man was stretched out on the couch, already snoring. "Silly man."

Wyatt made his way to their room and closed the door. He sat at the vid-screen and called Sebastian. The two men had grown extremely close once communications had opened up. They talked daily. They had so much in common, even though they were such different people. After a few minutes, the young man's face filled the screen.

"Wyatt," Sebastian said, smiling. "You look sleepy. How's the big celebration day going?"

"Exhausting. I ate so much food and talked to so many people. I'm done peopling." Sebastian snorted. "How are you guys? How was your and Leti's checkups with Nettle?"

"It went fine. Leti is still mad because his belly is bigger than mine, but we're both healthy. I'm due in two weeks, but Nets said she could come at any time."

"Two weeks! We won't be back in two weeks. I

thought you were a few weeks behind me and had until the end of the month. Sebastian, that means Alois won't be with you." Wyatt felt horrible. It was his fault everyone was still there. He had wanted to see things through on the planet. "It's my fault. I'm so sorry."

"Shut up," Sebastian said, rolling his eyes. "Alois is the lieutenant of a ship. He has responsibilities. We've already talked and it's fine. Leti's going to call him, then carry him around on his tablet. He won't physically be here, but he'll be here."

"I shouldn't have been so selfish," Wyatt said, covering his face.

"I'm sorry, but are you the captain of the Blue Sparrow? I recall Dru calling a vote on the matter and everyone, including Alois, voted to stay and see things through on Tammol. I even recall telling him that I thought he should vote to stay," Sebastian said. "Births are important, Wyatt, but so is saving a planet. Don't worry about Alois and me." A blush filled his cheeks.

"Hmm, how *are* you and Alois doing?"

"Oh my god, Wyatt," Sebastian said, closing his eyes and leaning his head back. "I think I'm in love. In person, it was too intense, but this long-distance thing? It was the best thing that could have happened. We talk every night and have since the day he left. We even exchanged messages through Jody during the time you all were offline. I've never known another person so well, not even Nina. I don't know if that would have happened if he had stayed here. I was so nervous and ashamed at the beginning."

"That's stupid," Wyatt said, snarling. "There's nothing for you to be ashamed of."

"I get that now. Having Leti, Shae, and you as friends has really helped me get my head on straight. I still have doubts, and I'm scared to death that he'll kiss me and we won't be mates, but I'm proud of myself. I love myself, damn it."

"That's as it should be," Wyatt said, nodding sharply. "How's the research going?"

"We have… ideas. Tomorrow night, we're gathering everyone together and presenting what we've discovered. It's pretty crazy, but it is what it is."

"Sounds like what happened here," Wyatt said softly. "Crazy."

"You really need to tell me the whole story. Alois has even been close-lipped about the whole thing."

"I will. It's just been so hectic, and I like talking about normal stuff with you. You know?"

"I get it. It's the same with me. What we've found is so horrifying, I just want to escape it for a bit," Sebastian said.

Wyatt sat up straight. "I just had a thought. What if we go into labor at the same time?"

Sebastian laughed. "We should make Alois be there with you with his tablet. He can experience it with me and you. The poor thing would pass out."

Wyatt giggled at the thought. Damn, he enjoyed their talks. Maybe Alois was right about there being no coincidences. Sebastian had helped him get through the past few months. He'd listened to him yap about everything from the local fauna to what Garen had cooked for dinner that night. They'd kept a running measure of their bellies and talked about nothing for hours. He missed Kiki so much, but it helped having Rune, Sebastian, and the others.

"What are you two giggling about in here?" Morgan rubbed his eyes and pressed a kiss to Wyatt's head.

"None of your business," Sebastian said, scowling. "Preggos only in this club."

"I'm a preggo," Leti's voice popped in through the comm. He darted behind Sebastian. "Hey, Wyatt." Leti's belly bump really was as big as Sebastian's.

"Hey," Wyatt said. "How're the kids? Do you need me to bring you another pet or baby?"

"No," Sebastian yelled. "His house is pure chaos now." He thought for a minute. "Well, maybe a teenager would be okay. They could help feed his menagerie."

Leti stuck his tongue out at his friend. "Mo already does that. My home is perfect. Lots of love, noise, and fun. How's Estella doing? Is she still set on coming home with you?"

"She is officially our adopted daughter," Morgan said, pride filling his eyes. "She still plans on being a doctor, like Wyatt."

"I talked to Nettle, and he said that as soon as she's old enough, he'll take her on as an apprentice until she goes to med school," Leti said. "Rizze and Mo can't wait to meet her. Sami and Pepper are indifferent."

"They're also babies. Sheesh," Sebastian said. "Shae finished setting up the nursery at Morgan's house. I seriously didn't realize how artistic he is. I'll send the pictures I took. He did this whole mural of the

Anchor's Rest System on the ceiling. Your girls are going to love it."

"It's not Morgan's house anymore," Leti said. "It's Wyatt and Morgan's home."

Wyatt leaned into Morgan's arms. He liked the sound of that.

"You all are welcome here any time," Rasha said, hugging Wyatt tightly. "I wish you didn't have to go, but I know your heart's home is on Charybdis Station." She pushed back and met his eyes. "Make sure the Lord Admiral knows we'll take any refugees that want to come. We need any and every occupation."

"I will," Wyatt said. "I plan on putting Leti on it. His father-in-law is basically putty in his hands. I'll miss you Rasha. I'm so damn proud of you and Dashel. You didn't just stop at taking care of our little group of Tammolians. I know you'll both be the best of leaders."

"We have Jody too," she said. "That woman is amazing."

"That she is."

"My turn." Dashel grabbed him and gave him a huge hug. "You always have a home here with us, Doc. Make sure you send us pictures of those babies when they come."

"I will," he promised, patting the man on the shoulder.

Jane waited next to them. "I know this is home now,

but I kind of wish we were going with you and Rune. I'm going to miss you so much."

"We've been together for years," he said, hugging her. He breathed in her familiar smell, wishing she was coming too. "Kiki and Joe, Rune, you and me."

"I wonder if Mr. Foster really cares that's he's lost two top notch medical teams. It's just the three of us now, and no one wants to even think of going back to the GACP."

"They let him go. He basically murdered our teams, and they just fined him," Wyatt said. "They don't deserve to have us."

"No, they don't," she said, hugging him one more time.

A few hours later, Wyatt watched Tammol disappear from the window in their room onboard the Blue Sparrow. His thoughts were still heavy. One downside of being connected to the galaxy again was learning that Ralen had never been tried for his actions. The GACP hadn't even tried. His family was apparently too influential. One good thing was that Ralen's uncle hadn't made it off Tammol. He'd died in the fighting.

Morgan's arms wrapped around him from behind. He couldn't reach all the way around Wyatt's belly, so his hands cupped Wyatt's baby bump. "We'll be on Rueal tonight. I can't believe I'm meeting your mom and stepdad. Do you know how scary that is?"

"Your stomach doesn't hurt though, does it?"

"No," he admitted, shrugging. "My ulcer must be gone."

"You never had an ulcer, baby. You've come a long way in accepting your position in Dru's crew," Wyatt said.

"Don't get all psychological on me, kitten."

He turned around and kissed his mate. "You're my big, responsible adult, aren't you?" he cooed.

18

SUGARWORM SYSTEM, PLANET RUEAL

A week later, Morgan watched the busy streets of Pagent's Distillery. Shuttles flew by and hundreds of people walked around. "Are you sure this is the right place?" Wyatt's stepdad, Jordan Adaden, stood beside him.

"Kiki made sure to send the address along with her list of the contents," Morgan said. He was not looking forward to packing up Kiki and Joe's cherished belongings. His mate still cried at night, missing his best friend. He'd caught Rune crying in the bathroom twice. Luna had even struggled for a while, looking for Kiki every time a door opened.

Jordan's hand was reassuring on Morgan's shoulder. "This is going to be shit, Morgan, but you need to do it. It's not likely you'll be back in this system again anytime soon."

"I know," Morgan sighed. "Damn it. It can't be worse than talking to Pela's folks." Her dads were good men. They'd both cried when he'd told them her last words.

Together, they crossed the street and entered the storage facility. There were lots of all sizes, ranging from just a couple of square feet to large rooms. He didn't know for sure what size Kiki's storage room was. A few minutes later, a manager led them to a large room, piled high with things.

"Oh, Kiki," Morgan said, running his hands along a wooden cradle. "Didn't plan to have kids, huh?"

"You want all of this moved to the spaceport? Our rates are down low right now if you don't want to take it all now," the manager said.

"No. We want it all moved," Morgan said. He looked around. There were a few pieces of furniture and a lot of crates. He would make sure they treasured the memories Kiki and Joe had collected here.

"Morgan, look," Jordan said. He held up a beautiful, handmade quilt. "Didn't Kiki write that this was her grandmother's? It's beautiful. There are so many precious, beautiful things in here."

This was why he'd asked the man to come with him. For the past two weeks, Wyatt's mom had been aloof and cold, at least toward Morgan. Jordan was the exact opposite. Morgan didn't think the man could be distant even if he tried. He was soft-hearted and a great big ball of sunshine.

"Wyatt will love it." Morgan signed the required paperwork, and they left, heading to a nearby café for a cup of coffee.

Jordan sighed happily as he sniffed his latte, then took a sip and watched Morgan for a few minutes.

"Sandra is a bit worried about you," he finally said. "I told her there wasn't anything to worry about, but she is damn protective of her boys."

"I won't hurt him," Morgan said, sipping his own coffee. "I love Wyatt more than anything in the galaxy. He, Estella, and the twins are the most important people to me."

Jordan looked thoughtful. "I think it's partly losing Verion. She loved him for a long time, still does to be honest. When Leti told her what happened, it sent her already well-developed protectiveness into overdrive. Then she had to deal with Wyatt being MIA. It's been hard on her. If she didn't have our boys, she would have been on a ship headed to Tammol to find him herself."

"He's safe now," Morgan said. "I don't get why she hates me."

"She doesn't hate you. She's wary of you."

"She doesn't need to be," Morgan said. "I'm not Jevio, and I will do anything to keep Wyatt and the kids safe."

"Like I said, it all goes back to Verion, at least partly. It took me a long time to convince her I was serious about her. She doesn't trust easily, especially when it concerns her heart or Wyatt's. She'll get there though. All you need to do is stay steady. That will prove your intentions."

"I can do that," Morgan said. "I'm not going anywhere."

"Sandra *was* a bit surprised to learn about the twins," Jordan said, stifling a laugh.

Morgan didn't even try to hide his laughter. "I thought her eyes were going to pop out of her head."

"You know how we live in the Boral System?"

"Yes," Morgan said, drawing out the word and tilting his head.

"Since she discovered she's going to be a grandmother, Sandra has been making noises about moving. I'm an engineer and can get work just about anywhere," Jordan said.

"Okay?"

"We know you two will make your home on Charybdis Station," he said.

"Yes?" Morgan wondered where the man was going with this.

"I already got a job on the station," Jordan said bluntly, watching him. "Leti arranged it. He even found us a nice house a few blocks away from yours."

Morgan blinked. Sandra would be close by. For the rest of their lives.

"Anything to say, son?"

"Fuck."

Jordan gave a full belly laugh. "At least it'll give you plenty of chances to prove yourself to her. We've already arranged for our things to be shipped."

"Well, I do like you and the boys," Morgan said, scowling. "Wyatt loves his mom."

"He does," Jordan agreed, eyes shining with laughter. "He loves you too. She'll figure that out."

His comm buzzed before he could think of anything to say. "Yes?"

"Morgan." Alois's panicked voice came through

clearly. His face perfectly matched his voice. "Wyatt's having the babies. Like right now. Holy shit!"

"What hospital?" Jordan asked, pulling Morgan's wrist to face him. Morgan couldn't move. Wyatt was having the babies.

"He refuses to go to any of them. He wants to have them on the ship. Rune and his mom are helping. What do you want me to do? Holy shit!"

"Calm down," Jordan said. "We're on our way back. Can I talk to Sandra?"

"Hey, honey," she said, peeking over Alois's shoulder. "You have time. His contractions just started."

"Great," Jordan said. "The kids excited?"

"They can't wait to meet their nieces. They're following their oldest niece around now," she said, amused. Wyatt's half-brothers were four and six, but they were convinced they had to protect all their nieces, eight-year-old Estella included.

"We'll be there soon. I got to get this lug moving."

"He doesn't want to come, does he? Is labor too inconvenient for him?" Sandra was pissed.

"No, babe," Jordan said, softly. "He's frozen. Has been since Alois said the babies were coming. I think it's new daddy panic. Look." He turned Morgan's comm back to face him.

Morgan still couldn't move. His kitten was having the babies.

"Oh, my," Sandra said, chuckling. "Pale and shaking is not a good look on him."

"It's really not," Alois said, pale and shaking too. "Holy shit!"

Jordan stood and pulled him to his feet. "Come on, daddy. Let's get you to the ship before the babies get there."

"Wyatt," Morgan said, suddenly mobile. "I need to get to Wyatt."

SEVEN HOURS LATER, Kiki and Pela Morrick were born. Morgan sat next to Wyatt and held little Kiki. "Look at her ears! They're so adorable. Look at her toes. Look at these little toes!"

"You are such a domesticated dork." Leti laughed through the screen of Alois's tablet. The Dedril had it strapped to his chest, letting Leti, Shae, and Sebastian see the babies. "I really didn't see it in you, Morgan, but you're a family man now."

"He's going to be a good daddy," Rune said, smiling. He worked on cleaning up the med-bay.

"She's my angel," Morgan whispered.

"What about Pela?" Wyatt was tired, but his eyes were so full of joy.

"I have two angels," Morgan said. "Let me see my Pela." They switched babies, and he admired his little girl. "They have so much hair. I didn't think babies had that much hair."

Sandra rested her hand on his shoulder, smiling at him. "Wyatt had a full head of hair when he was born too. Runs in the family, I guess."

"Can we come in now?" Estella asked from the

door. Her curly hair was a halo around her head. Morgan had three angels. Damn, he was lucky.

"Yes, sweetie," Morgan said. "Come meet your sisters."

Sandra hugged him, and he stiffened. What the fuck?

"You are going to be such a good daddy," she said, tears in her eyes. "I'm sorry I was such a jerk, Morgan."

"You were just being protective," he said softly. "It's fine."

"They're so tiny," Estella said.

"They'll grow fast," Leti said. "Pepper sprouted like a little weed. Enjoy the new baby smell while you can, guys. After that, it's just poopy diapers and hair pulling."

"Sebastian," Alois said. "Did you see all of that? You're going to do that. You two made little people. In your bodies. Holy shit!"

"Hmm," Sebastian said. "I'm starting to think it might be a good thing for you to be on a screen when Nina is born."

"He would totally faint," Shae said. "If Jordan hadn't caught him, he would have fainted there."

"Okay," Alois said. "I think it's time Wyatt got some sleep, so you three need to go."

"Alois," the three whined in unison.

"Goodbye," he said and clicked the tablet off.

"You do need to rest, baby boy," Sandra said, wiping Sebastian's forehead. "Sleep for a bit. We'll watch your girls."

"Lie with me, Morgan?"

"Nothing I'd rather do," he said and handed Pela to Jordan. He stretched out alongside Wyatt, wrapping his arms around his mate. He had never felt so much happiness at once. "Estella, come give us some love before you go."

The little girl reluctantly left Kiki's side. Wyatt's brothers were cooing at Pela, completely ignoring their older sibling. Estella kissed Wyatt's cheek and flicked Morgan's nose. "I love you guys. I gotta go spoil my sisters now." She followed Wyatt's family out the door.

"Morgan, can I talk to you for a minute?" Alois poked his head back in the door.

"Okay," he said. "Be right back," he told Wyatt. "Rune! You have cuddle duty."

"On it," Rune said, sliding into the bed to hold Wyatt.

Dru, Quinn, and Hazel were with Alois in the hall. "There's a situation," Dru said.

"What's wrong?"

"Ralen Jevio is in the spaceport with city enforcers. He says he has full custody of the twins. I checked, and he has the paperwork," she said, face red with anger.

"Fuck him," Morgan said, growling. "I'm not giving my girls to that fucker."

"Yeah," Alois said. "That's not happening, no matter what."

"I agree," Dru said. "The thing is, he has the paperwork according to the government of Rueal."

"What do we do? Do you want me to kill him?" Quinn looked a little too eager.

"Oh, he'll die soon enough. I already put a contract in with Half-Moon," Dru said. "I promised Kiki."

"I called Foster," Hazel blurted out. She danced nervously from foot to foot. "I thought he might be able to help. He should be here any minute."

"Why did you do that? What can he do?" Alois asked. "He didn't even see the trial through."

"I can do quite a bit actually." Behind them, Foster stood with Lerais. "The reason I didn't press for a trial was because I was afraid for Wyatt's children. I made an agreement with the Jevio family. They promised to leave Wyatt and his children alone in return for settling privately with my company."

"That didn't work out so well, did it?" Quinn said, voice thick with sarcasm.

"No, it didn't, but they broke their agreement, so I can break mine," he said. "My lawyers have contacted Enforcement, and I've sent the media every speck of proof we have against Ralen. It should be streaming right about now."

Alois turned his tablet on and spun it around, grinning. "Look at this."

A stern-faced newswoman was in the middle of reporting Jevio's actions. "After learning that his lover, Dr. Wyatt Morrick, was pregnant, Ralen Jevio, son of Michael and Janeen Jevio, refused to extract his team, which directly led to the deaths of five of the eight people on the medical team aiding the planet Tammol. Here's a recording of his call with Dr. Morrick."

Jevio's face filled the screen, ugly with his anger and disgust.

Fuck you, Wyatt. I'm not losing my inheritance because your pathetic hybrid ass got pregnant. You won't kill it? Fine. I'll make sure you and the spawn never make it off that fucking planet. Hope you enjoyed this call, because I'm cutting communications with the planet now. Uncle Berenit's friends are going to fuck it all to hell soon enough.

"As you can see," the newswoman continued, "Jevio's intentions were to kill Dr. Wyatt and his unborn child. Jevio prevented the team from leaving the planet, knowing his uncle would be aiding the Concord mercenaries in attacking it."

Kiki, Pela, Joe, Lolani, and Ron's photos appeared on the screen.

"These five people died on the planet, along with the majority of the Tammolian people. We're joining Ben Cordell at the Pagent's Distillery Spaceport now. Jevio and his parents signed an agreement with the GACP that said he would stay away from Dr. Morrick and any child or children he had in return for a private settlement. He is currently in the process of breaking that agreement."

"Hi, Betsy," Ben Cordell said, smiling face filling the corner of the screen. "We're at the Pagent's Distillery Spaceport now where Ralen Jevio is demanding custody of Dr. Wyatt Morrick's newborn daughters. They were born only three hours ago. Mr. Jevio? Why do want custody of the children? You referred to them as spawn when learning of Dr. Morrick's pregnancy."

Ralen Jevio stood with a ring of enforcers. The enforcer standing at his side spoke into his comm, ignoring the commotion.

Ralen hid his face with his hand. "Get out of my face. This is my business."

"Do you plan to murder them since you didn't succeed in killing Dr. Morrick when he was pregnant?"

"I don't know what you're talking about," Ralen said, outraged.

"Okay, guys. Orders are to leave Morrick alone," the lead enforcer said. "Ralen Jevio, you are under arrest for the murder of five employees of the GACP and for complicity in the attempted genocide of the Tammolian race."

"*What?*" Jevio was roughly turned around and cuffed.

Ben Cordell peppered him with questions as they dragged him to the shuttle.

"Oh," Dru said, pleased. "That was just so pretty."

"Why did you settle in the first place?" Quinn watched Foster curiously. "This drama could have already been over."

"After watching the recording, I was afraid Ralen's family would do their best to make the children disappear. I know them, and they are human purists. I thought Ralen was different," Foster said. "I talked it over with Lolani, Ron, and Pela's families before I offered the settlement. They wanted justice but were worried about the babies too."

"Pela's dads didn't say anything when I talked to them last week," Morgan said. "I didn't even think about Jevio trying to hurt the girls."

"This should be a time of celebration for you, so don't worry. I'll take care of things here," Foster said, looking around. "If you can though, go ahead and leave the planet. I don't want those babies to be used as tools in this thing."

"I finished the final repairs to the ship this morning," Lerais said. "We're ready to go."

"I'll go talk to Wyatt's mom and stepdad now," Morgan said. He grabbed Foster, hugging the man. "Thank you. I didn't want to have to fight our way off the planet."

"No problem," he squeaked. Maybe Morgan was hugging him a bit too tightly. Oops.

"We'll leave immediately if Wyatt's family is okay with it. They're already staying with us, and the storage place delivered Kiki and Joe's things already," Dru said.

"Let's get home," Morgan said, setting Foster back on his feet.

19

EN ROUTE TO SILVERLIGHT SYSTEM, DESTINATION CHARYBDIS STATION

"*L*eti, Shae, and Sebastian won't take my calls," Wyatt said. "It's been a week. Do you think they're mad at me?"

Morgan growled. They'd better not be. His mate was fucking perfect, and Morgan hated seeing the doubt in his eyes. He carefully worked on combing through Estella's wild hair, ready to try to braid it again. He had finally brought himself to share his conditioner with his daughter, and her soft hair was much more manageable.

"They don't seem the type, Wyatt," Rune said, cuddling Kiki. "Hell, Leti even said I could live with him when we get to Charybdis Station, so they can't possibly be mad at you. It's not their way. There's probably another reason. They did their presentation about that artifact thingy the other day, so maybe things just picked up for them on the station."

"You're probably right. It's just weird. Sebastian and

I talk every morning before he heads over to Leti's house," Wyatt said.

He finished changing Pela's diaper and wrapped her up like a burrito. He kissed her soft head and laid her down in the wooden cradle that had belonged to Kiki and Joe. Morgan could watch them all day.

"Rune, you know you're living with Morgan and me, right?"

"Does Morgan know that?" Rune gave him a teasing wink.

Morgan rolled his eyes and ignored the man. Luna sat on his foot, grinning at him. "Try not to worry too much. I'll call Selene in a minute and see if anything is going on," Morgan said. His eyes shifted to Wyatt again. "Or you could call her."

"No!"

"Why don't you want to meet Selene, kitten?"

"You didn't want to meet Mom," Wyatt said accusingly. "I should be able to not want to meet your Selene."

"What's the deal? She's just another member of the Blue Solace. I talked to her the other day, and she seems nice," Rune said.

"She has basically been his family since he was ten," Wyatt said. "She's his big sister and he adores her. Then there's Ma and Pops."

"What?" Rune looked at Morgan.

"After my parents died, I didn't really have anywhere to go, so I lived on the streets on Union Station for a few years. Hack's first mission as a captain was on the planet. While they were there, I tried to steal one of Selene's vibro-swords. Needless to say, she caught me, then brought me to Ma and Pops in Charybdis."

"Aww, Wyatt doesn't want to meet your sister and your parents," Rune said, laughing.

"Fine. I'll call her," Wyatt said, scowling. "Rude people." Morgan watched him try to call Selene on the vid-screen. "She's not answering either. What's going on?"

Morgan worked on braiding Estella's hair while he thought. "It's probably a mission of some kind. There may have been a Concord attack. Hmm, usually, Sebastian will still answer though."

"I'm worried," Wyatt said. "We're entering the Silverlight System today, but we're still a good two weeks away."

"Sebastian's having the baby!" Alois ran inside, his tablet held above his head. Luna jumped to her feet, barking. "Look, look!"

"Can you guys calm him down," Leti asked with a laugh. Morgan could see him sitting next to Sebastian's bed, holding his hand.

"Come here, Alois," Wyatt said, pulling the man onto a couch by the window. Luna jumped next to Alois and peered over his shoulder. "Let's see how Sebastian's doing, okay?"

"Yeah. That's good," Alois said. He had been a wreck while Wyatt was giving birth, but he looked like shit now. Worry and fear made him pale, and he was in complete disarray.

"He's doing great, Alois," Leti said. "Nettle and his

whole medical team are here, so you know he's in good hands. Hack and the rest of the crew are waiting in the next room. We're here for your man."

"I'm here for your man too, Sebastian," Wyatt said. "It will hurt like hell, but it's so worth it."

Morgan finished braiding Estella's hair. With Rune's help, he took Luna and the kids to get lunch and kept them busy for the next few hours. He made sure to check in on his mate and friend, grinning at Alois's ever-changing expressions. He knew just what the man was feeling.

Wyatt stayed next to Alois and held his hand the whole time Sebastian gave birth. Around the ten-hour point, Alois ran in to the commons, waving his tablet again at Morgan and the rest of the crew who were sitting eating dinner.

"Look at her," he said, awe covering his face. "Look at my girl."

Sebastian laughed from the screen as Alois passed the tablet around. He held a little bundled baby girl. She was clearly a hybrid, with pointy ears and soft lavender skin. Two little grey, stubby horns poked through her downy head of hair.

"Since we don't know who her father is, they tested her, and she is a mixture of Wello, Siren, Silet, Havonite, and Human. Isn't she adorable?" Sebastian's eyes were stuck to his daughter. He was clearly in love.

"She's perfect," Alois said.

"That is one pretty baby," Dru agreed. "You did good, Seb."

"Does that mean you want a baby, Dru?" Leti's voice was all innocence.

"Hell no! I'm the fun aunt. That's it," Dru said.

"I don't know," Lerais said, holding Pela and rocking her. "Babies are awful cute."

"No. We have Monty," she said, pointing at the newt perched on her shoulder. "That's enough."

"You'd make such pretty babies, Dru," Sebastian said.

"I hate you all." She scowled and leaned into Lerais's side to admire Pela. "Babies are cute, but it's best when you can give them back to their parents when they stink too much."

"You have a point," Lerais said, wrinkling his nose and handing Pela to Sandra. "Here's your granddaughter."

Leti shook his head. "Shameful." His happy, exhausted face grew serious. "Everything happened all at once here, but the last week has been crazy. I need to tell you all some things, but we need everyone there and this isn't really the time. Dru, can you all plan a conference call in a few hours?"

"Of course," she said, frowning. "Is it bad?"

"It's... confusing," Leti said.

Morgan left the commons and went back to their room. Wyatt looked exhausted. Luna and he were curled up on the couch, wrapped in one of Kiki's quilts. He had a silly, happy smile on his face. "We are so having eight kids," Wyatt said. "I'm already forgetting how much birth hurts."

Morgan slipped in behind him, and Wyatt settled

his head on Morgan's arm.

"Hmm, can we count Rune and your brothers as three of them? Then we'll have six already," Morgan said.

"Nope." Wyatt kissed his arm. "We only have three. That means five more. As soon as I'm up to it, we'll get to work."

"And you say I'm the romantic one," Morgan said, kissing his head.

———

THE SMALL CONFERENCE room was packed. Everyone except Jordan was there since Wyatt's stepdad was given baby-sitting duty. Wyatt sat between Morgan and Rune, and Morgan wrapped an arm around his shoulders. He had a bad feeling about this call. It didn't make him feel any better to see Lord Admiral Fasi Juren's grim face next to Leti's on the screen.

"We have a lot of information to give you all," the Lord Admiral said. "As you all know, Leti, Sebastian, and Shae have been researching the artifact that Dr. Verion Morrick came across. We knew the Concords wanted it, but we didn't know why." He gestured to Leti. "Go ahead and tell them, son."

Leti sighed, meeting Wyatt's eyes. "I'm sorry for all this, Wyatt." He took a big breath and let it out. "Okay. The artifact is one of seven that we are aware of. They each house a living, sentient being in gaseous form. Within the artifacts, I don't think the beings can do anything or communicate. However, the Ancient Crells had rituals that allowed these beings to move into living hosts."

"Whoa," Dru said. "That was unexpected."

"I know, right?" Fasi looked disturbed. "You don't know the half of it either."

"These beings have existed for a very long time. When the seven beings are given bodies, they warred with every nearby people or world. Ultimately, they drove the Crells to their own destruction," Leti said. "I'm sending my full report to you all so you can take your time and read over it."

"Thanks," Alois said. "Now what does this all have to do with us?"

"The seven beings are the Queen, Life, Death, Water, Fire, Air, and Earth," Leti said.

"They sound like a band," Quinn said, frowning.

Leti smiled at the woman, then continued. "The Queen rules them completely. I don't know what her full powers are, but in the past, she controlled the others without a doubt. The other six are her weapons. They each have unique gifts that made conquering everything in her path easy," Leti said. "We have reason to believe that at least some of these beings have bodies. A group of archeologists woke them up somehow. Now, we suspect the Queen took over Dr. Linda Belcort's body, Life took her husband, and Earth her daughter. We have surveillance of them building a compound on a planet in the Crellic System that is supposed to be dead."

"Are they connected to the Concords somehow?" Morgan asked. The Concords had always been assholes, but over the last year, they had become organized assholes with a purpose.

"Yes," Fasi said. "Life has been working with them and is very likely leading them."

"What can he do? What's Life's special powers?" Hazel asked.

"He and Death are the Queen's right and left hands. Life can control minds," Leti said. "There must be some small bit of consent given, but in all the histories, he's a trickster. He offers a person what they want. Once they accept it, their mind becomes his. He can literally control whole armies."

"Shit," Lerais said. "That's rough."

"Yes," Leti said simply. "Shae managed to see a bit of Life's work on a few of the Concords we've come across. It's crazy. He made some that were captured stop breathing. They just stopped."

"Fuck. This war just got a lot more complicated," Dru said. "What about Earth?"

"Earth builds the Queen's empire and controls her slaves. At this point, both the Queen and Earth are on Genarg in the Crellic System," Leti said.

"What about the others?" Wyatt asked. "Fire, Air, Water, and Death." He tapped away at his tablet, reading the documents Leti had sent.

"Fire is the easiest to understand. He burns things to ash. Air is weird. I think he will have to be planet-side to be a danger. He's able to create massive storms and devastate planets that way. I think he can use air to rip things apart too. I suspect that's what happened to Belcort's son. Water…"

"Oh fuck, fuck, fuck," Wyatt said, interrupting Leti. "I'll be right back." He jumped from his chair and ran out of the room. Luna darted after him.

Everyone stared at the door. "Maybe he had to use the bathroom," Rune said, shrugging.

"Okay," Leti said. "Anyway, Water is able to control any fluid within range of its senses, and from what I read, he has a long range."

"Oh," Rune said, looking back at the door. "We met him, I think, on Tammol. The Concords' creature."

"What are you talking about? You all have been hush-hush about something that happened there," Fasi said.

"It was crazy," Dru said. "The Concords had a creature working for them. It looked and acted like a human, but it was able to drain the fluids from the population of whole cities at once. He was the one that killed most of the Tammolians. We recorded some of the damage it caused. I'm sending it now." She grabbed her tablet. "I'm sorry I didn't give details in the report."

"The details you gave were crazy enough," Fasi said. "I understand wanting to put it out of your mind. What happened to it?"

Wyatt strode back in and held up a small pyramid shaped artifact that looked a whole lot like the one that his father had found. "Kiki and Pela killed it with a poison I developed. The creature could heal any wound given to it, though we didn't try decapitation. No one could get close enough to do that. Our friend Dashel found this near its remains."

"Hold it a little closer," Leti said, squinting. "That's

Water's container."

"Well, that's one of the fuckers down," Morgan said. "Wyatt's poison was able to kill it."

Leti grinned. "Plus, you have its container, so it can't be placed in a new host." He cheered, whooping loudly. "This is good news, guys. Really good news."

"There is still bad news to give, son," Fasi said, hand on Leti's shoulder.

The man slumped down. "Yeah. There is. So, the artifact your father found contained Death. He seems to be the most powerful of the Elements. Based on my readings and our experiences, he must be placed in a dead host while the others are placed in living hosts. His powers are extensive. He can basically freeze time or speed it up. The more fanciful tales say he can collect the souls of anyone within his range of senses, leaving behind empty, living shells."

"You have his container though, right?" Dru looked worried, and Morgan didn't blame her, imagining another, more dangerous Water.

"No," Leti said. "Dr. Franklin used it to provide Death with a host. She failed twice, but the third time worked. Franklin's dead now, but Death is currently entering the Silverlight System."

"Oh no," Dru said. "I guess he's going to the Crellic System?"

"That's our best guess," Fasi said. He poked Leti in the shoulder.

The young man grimaced. "The body Franklin used was your dad's, Wyatt. I'm so sorry. Death is walking around in your dad's body."

20

Wyatt paced back and forth in the small bathroom attached to their room. Estella was asleep on one of the couches with Luna, and the twins had just settled down. He didn't want to keep anyone awake, but he couldn't sleep. Too many things rolled around his head. He had finally finished the last of his dad's letters, and his heart was so close to breaking.

I love you more than all the stardust in the galaxy.

He came to a stop, propping his head on the mirror. He looked down at all the hair products his mate had strewn over the bathroom cabinet. His beautiful mate. He closed his eyes. His dad was dead, but not.

There were so many possibilities, even if Leti seemed certain that Verion Morrick no longer lived. His soul was drawn back to his body, so that meant that he was in there somewhere, right? Being a medical doctor sure as shit hadn't prepared him for this.

"Kitten, you need to get some rest," Morgan said,

slipping inside the bathroom. Wyatt turned around and threw himself against his mate. Morgan grunted but caught him, pulling him close. "This is some shit, huh?"

"I have to go after him, Morgan," Wyatt said. "I have to."

"It's too dangerous. We have Estella and the twins to think about. We can't bring them into a warzone. Well, not if we can help it."

"I know," he said quietly. "I know you're right. I love them so much. Estella is such a brave, smart girl. I never expected her." He rubbed his face against Morgan's soft shirt. "The twins are such a special gift. I hate that I let Ralen touch me, but I got those two angels out of it."

"We have a damn good family, kitten," Morgan said. "That's for sure."

"Our family," he said with wonder. "Ours."

"I love you," Morgan said. "Why are you so surprised?"

"I'm not," Wyatt said. He really wasn't. He was as certain of Morgan's love as he was of his own. "They're ours though. We're a family."

"Yeah," Morgan said, chuckling. "Nice time for it to sink in."

"Marry me," Wyatt said. The words flew out of his mouth. He looked into his mate's eyes. "Marry me. Take my name. Today. Right now."

"Right now?" Morgan looked shell-shocked. "Are you sure? You don't want to wait for a nice, big wedding at Charybdis Station?"

"I don't need that. If you want a big wedding, we

can have one too, but I want you to be mine. Right now."

"Kitten, I was yours the second I saw your picture," Morgan said, kissing him softly. "It becomes more real every time I see you, hear you, breathe in your scent." He nuzzled Wyatt's neck. "Every time I'm inside of you and feel your body moving with mine." He cupped Wyatt's face, his eyes intense. "I'm yours, Wyatt."

"I'm yours too, Morgan. Marry me," he asked.

"I will," Morgan answered him. "First thing in the morning. You want Estella there, right?"

"Yeah," Wyatt said, sulking. He wanted it right now. Stupid people and their need for sleep.

"I'm awake," Estella said, face poking in the bathroom. "I heard you guys. Let's get married right now, Morgan. It's the perfect time."

"That's my girl," Wyatt said, pushing Morgan away and pulling his daughter in for a hug.

Morgan laughed. "Fine, kitten. Let's wake everyone up."

"I'm calling Sebastian," he said, trying to stay quiet so he didn't wake the twins.

"They're awake too," Estella said, peeking into Pela's crib. "I'll go get Gramma and Grampa."

Wyatt turned the lights on and checked on the girls. They stared at him with big brown eyes. Pretty girls. He turned and called Sebastian.

"What's going on? Why are you calling so late, Wyatt?" Sebastian yawned. "Do you need to talk about your dad?"

"I'm getting married," he said. "Right now. Morgan

and Estella have gone to fetch the crew and my parents. Are you really tired? Having babies tends to make a person tired."

"I'm not tired enough to miss your wedding," Sebastian said. "I need to call the others. They'll want to be there for Morgan. Give me an hour."

"I guess," Wyatt grumbled.

An hour later, a huge crowd gathered on one of vid-screens in the commons. The Lord Admiral and his wife were smashed between two large Grell.

"Oh, my baby is getting married," Ma sniffled, wiping her eyes. "He's a doctor too. It's so nice to meet you, darling."

Pops grinned from ear to ear. "Our pretty boy found himself a mate. How many babies did you want to have again, Wyatt?"

"Eight is what Morgan said," Selene said. "That seems excessive, but you two are Morgan's role models."

"He already has three. I'd say that's a good start," Jane said. She and Garen were on another vid-screen along with Dashel, Rasha, and their other friends from Tammol. "You look beautiful, Wyatt. I love your wedding pajamas."

"Okay. Everyone shut up," Dru said, growling. "I want to get back to bed."

"Morgan wants to get back to bed too," Hack said, waggling his brows.

"I said shut up," Dru said. "Now, are you two ready?"

"Yes, sir," they both said.

"Fuck. Let's do this. So, marriage is important and stuff," Dru said.

"This is so beautiful," Selene said, voice flat and empty.

"Dru *is* pure eloquence," Rasha added.

"Two people have to really care about each other to make it work," Dru said, sending the vid-screens a dirty look. "You're going to get sick of each other at some point. It happens."

"Wow," Leti said. "We should have had Dru do our wedding, Will."

Wyatt bit his lip, trying not to laugh. Dru rolled her eyes and ignored them all. "To be happy, you need to make sure that you keep doing shit together. Don't just do your own thing. On the other hand, you also need to be your own person. No one likes a needy asshole."

"Needy asshole? There are so many things I could say right now," Lucas said, squeezing his eyes shut. "Don't say it, don't say it."

"Each of you will add something to the other's life. Something special. Don't take that for granted, okay?" Dru stared them down until they both nodded. "You two also need to stay honest with each other. Don't hide shit from each other. That only leads to someone getting their dick hurt."

"What if they like getting their dick hurt?" Draif looked curious. "Don't kink shame, Dru."

"I *said* shut the fuck up," Dru warned. "Okay, so Morgan, you good to do this? You agree to marry your mate and take damn good care of him?"

"Uh, is this where I say *I do*?" Morgan looked

puzzled, and a snicker escaped Wyatt. He pressed his lips hard together.

"Obviously, son," Pops said. "Go on."

"Oh, okay. I do," Morgan said. He slid Kiki's gold wedding band onto Wyatt's finger. Wyatt thought of her and Joe – their happiness and passion.

"Finally," Dru said. "Wyatt, are you sure you want to marry pretty boy here? There's no better guy out there, but he's probably going to be kind of high maintenance."

"Oh dear," Ma said, sniffling. "His hair gunk does cost an awful lot. He loves his hair."

"I do," Wyatt said solemnly. "I'm a doctor so I can afford your pricey haircare products, baby." He slid Joe's wedding ring on Morgan's finger, admiring the evidence of his claim. Joe would have liked Morgan a lot.

"There you go," Dru said. She tossed her hands in the air and shimmied. "You two are married. Of course, it's not legal until you file the paperwork, but whatever."

"My baby is married to a doctor," Ma said, sobbing. "It's all so magical."

WYATT'S PARENTS were borrowing Hazel's room for the trip and had agreed to take the kids so Wyatt and Morgan could have a little privacy on their wedding night.

"I'm sorry we can't have sex," Wyatt said. "In about three more weeks, we'll be good to go."

"Hmm," Morgan said, prowling closer to Wyatt. "Sex isn't just my dick in your ass, kitten."

Wyatt blushed. "I'm not good at *that* though." They had made love hundreds of times, but he hadn't gathered the courage to offer Morgan his mouth. He sure as shit liked Morgan's mouth on him though.

"Did Jevio tell you that?" Morgan looked disgruntled.

"Maybe," Wyatt said.

His mate's eyes softened. "Would you try it? For me? If you don't like it, then we won't do it, but if you don't want to because Jevio told you that you were bad at it, that's different."

"Okay," Wyatt agreed. He'd been thinking about what Morgan would taste like. He could trust Morgan. He could do this. Morgan kissed him, pulling him to the bed, and they fell onto it. They kissed and moved against each other, slipping out of their clothes. Wyatt blinked. Morgan's cock bobbed inches from his face. He mouth actually started watering.

"If you don't want to, that's fine." Morgan's voice rumbled, building in his chest.

Wyatt grunted, and Morgan gently cradled his head in his hands.

"Open up, kitten," he said and nudged his mouth with the head of his cock.

Wyatt hummed with pleasure and licked the tip of Morgan's dick. *Yum*, he thought. He opened his mouth wide, swallowing deep. He had thought about this so much but had never been able to imagine his husband's taste. Morgan tasted so damn good. Wyatt couldn't help but moan around Morgan's dick.

As he moved his mouth up and down, he reached out to squeeze Morgan's heavy balls. His husband groaned and began to thrust his hips, hands holding Wyatt's head still while he fucked his mouth. Wyatt's mouth was full of Morgan, salty and spicy. His body burned, and he felt a tug on his cock. Morgan stroked him, slowly, matching his strokes with his thrusts. Wyatt moaned around the dick in his mouth, and Morgan grunted and thrust faster.

Morgan's hand pumped quickly, and suddenly, Wyatt was there. He felt his body explode, and he shuddered. His cum covered Morgan's fingers, his moans rumbling around Morgan's cock, until his husband shouted and his seed slid down Wyatt's throat. He struggled to swallow every drop and continued to suck and nibble at Morgan's softening cock.

"Jevio was an idiot, kitten," Morgan said, voice sleepy. "I'm not an idiot."

Wyatt crawled up Morgan's body and settled his head on his husband's shoulder. "You're my husband now."

"Damn right I am," Morgan said. "I will always be here for you, kitten. No matter what. Even if it means chasing down your dad's body."

21

SILVERLIGHT SYSTEM, PLANET UNION STATION

A couple of weeks passed in quiet as the Blue Sparrow sped quickly through the Silverlight System, finally landing at Union Station to resupply and meet up with Charybdis Station's Green General, Caspian Juren.

Wyatt fed Kiki, watching as his daughter guzzled her milk down. Her hair had darkened quite a bit in the last few weeks. He suspected she'd have Ralen's black curls. He couldn't make himself mind though. His daughter belonged to Wyatt and Morgan, and they would make sure she grew into a wonderful person. It didn't matter who she looked like.

"Damn, you look beautiful," Morgan said, looking straight at him. He sat on the couch and rocked Pela. Their other daughter already looked just like Wyatt. She had a stubby little nose and mousy-brown hair. She also had a good set of lungs.

"You're a bit biased," Wyatt said. He made kissy faces at his husband. "You looove me."

Estella laughed. "You guys are so weird." She sat on the floor, reading a medical textbook on his tablet. Luna sprawled beside the girl, snoring softly, while Nugget curled into her side.

"You're reading my old pediatrics textbook, and you call *us* weird?" Wyatt said, shaking his head.

"What were you reading when you were my age?" Estella eyed him knowingly.

He winced. "Fine. I was reading my dad's old college textbooks."

"This family is too smart for me," Morgan said. He made silly faces at Pela. "You're going to be super smart too. Even Luna's smarter than me."

"Hmm," Wyatt said. "She did know better than to eat that expired MRE. Unlike you."

"It's okay, Morgan," Estella said. "You're super smart in your own way. You may give yourself food poisoning, but you keep tricking Quinn and Hazel into training harder. You're clever and sneaky."

"He really is," Wyatt agreed, bending to kiss the top of Estella's head. "He's smart and funny. Kind and goofy. He's good with hair too. Your curls are gorgeous, sweetheart." They fell down her back, smooth and silky. Her brown horns poked up through them, gleaming in the light. "It just took him months to figure it out."

"I feel so loved," Morgan said, rolling his eyes. He put Pela back in her crib, then plopped back on the couch, stretching his long legs out. "Are you excited about going to the market with your gramma?"

"Yes," Estella said excitedly. "I'm going to buy a new

dress. I want to look pretty when we get to Charybdis Station. Everyone will be there, and Mo said he'd take me to look at some of the gardens."

"Mo," Morgan said, growling low.

Wyatt laughed at him. "He's just her friend, Morgan, calm down. She's not even thinking about boys or girls that way yet."

"What way?" Estella looked at them, puzzled.

"See?" Wyatt sat next to his husband and unclenched his mate's bunched fists. "Plus, she's only eight, and he just turned thirteen."

"Estella, you can never date, alright?"

She shrugged. "If it will make you feel better, then okay."

Morgan smiled, smug and happy. "That's my girl."

"Hey," Jordan said, strolling through the open door to their room. "Are you ready to go shopping, sweetheart?"

"Yes!" Estella jumped up and ran for the door.

"Shoes, sweetie," Morgan said. He jumped up and pulled the stroller out of the closet. "Are you all sure you're alright with taking the twins too? That's two babies, a toddler, a six-year-old, and an eight-year-old to take care of in a busy market."

"We'll be fine," Jordan said. "Rune and Hazel are going to come with us too. They insisted since the Concords have access to the planet. That's four adults to five kids. Of course, Estella here is a good girl, so she's not a worry anyway."

"I'll watch out for Georgy and Maro too," she said.

She loved her uncles, even if they always tried to boss her around.

"Come on, darling," Jordan said, pushing the stroller out the door. "We have dresses to shop for."

"Does he really like shopping?" Morgan picked Wyatt's tablet up from the floor and refilled Luna's water bowl.

"Not at all," Wyatt said with a laugh. "He hates it more than anything in the world, but if Estella or Mom want to go, he'll go. He's a better man than me."

"Me too," Morgan said. "You ready to meet with Cas and the rest of them? We have about fifteen minutes."

"I want to cuddle," Wyatt said. He pushed Morgan back until his mate fell on the couch. "We can sit in the quiet and cuddle."

"Anything you want, kitten."

WYATT WATCHED the video in disbelief. Cas fidgeted in his seat, squirming. He kept darting looks Wyatt's way. "As you all see, Death didn't head for the Crellic System like we thought. He went to his old lab on Frost Veil."

"He killed Franklin too," Dru said, grimacing. "Not that she didn't deserve it, but it doesn't make much sense."

Wyatt's lip trembled as he watched his dad walk into snow, barefoot. He wore a sheet wrapped around his waist and nothing else. He had to be cold, but he didn't even flinch. His bone-white skin and hair looked garish in the sunlight. He had to be so cold. Wyatt sniffed.

"Damn it," Cas said, leaping from his chair. He picked Wyatt up and crushed him in a giant hug. "You poor thing. I'm so sorry about your dad. You don't have to watch this if you don't want to. Okay?"

Morgan cleared his throat. "That's my husband, Cas. Just so you know."

"I can't help it, Morgan. He sniffled," Cas said, sniffling himself.

"You okay, kitten?"

"Yes," Wyatt said, face squished against Cas' chest. "He's warm and soft. I like it. Can we keep him?"

"Will he count toward our eight kids?"

"I guess," Wyatt answered. "Though that's not really fair."

"Put him down, Cas," Dru said, exasperated. "They *will* adopt you. Wyatt isn't quite as bad as Leti, but it's too close for comfort."

Cas finally let him go, and Wyatt missed his warmth.

"Hmph! Fine." Wyatt stomped back to his seat. "Dad went to Frost Veil because he's still Dad, at least to some degree."

"His eyes aren't his eyes, Wyatt," Lerais said softly. "They're completely black like in all the drawings and records Leti showed us."

"Maybe so, but he's at Frost Veil. The place he spent most of his life. He's killing the Concord ships that approach but freezing Charybdis Station's. He *is* Death. I can't argue that, but he's also Dad."

"That doesn't match with the others," Cas said. "Life showed no sign of retaining anything, knowledge or emotions, from Dr. Windell Belcort. Leti's friend at the university on Siletus said that the Belcorts' daughter was lazy and hated dirt, but we have records showing her covered in mud, overseeing the workers on Genarg. If Life and Earth retain nothing from their hosts, why would Death?"

"He has a point, Wyatt," Morgan said, squeezing his hand. "We don't know anything about Water's previous host, but the way the Concords reacted to him suggests he didn't have any humanity left in him."

"There is one thing," Cas said hesitantly.

"What?" Wyatt knew his father was in there somewhere. He knew it.

"The Concords are agitated. Majorly."

"Well, a lot of them were killed on Tammol," Linc said. "That would upset them, right?" Nugget's face peeked over the table, watching everyone. The cat was getting big. Linc rubbed her head, and a purr rumbled through her. "Plus, they lost Water. That had to be a blow."

"True, but this is recent. It started around the time Death got to Frost Veil, which makes me think it has something to do with him," Cas said. "I wish we could track the others."

"We don't even know if Fire and Air have hosts yet," Dru said. "I'd like to say they don't, since we haven't seen them, but we don't hear everything that goes on in the galaxy. Plus, I don't think Charybdis is high on the Queen's radar. At least not yet."

"There's a lot we don't know," Cas said. "I do know that the Concords are flooding Silverlight System ever since Death landed on Frost Veil."

"He's killing them though," Wyatt said. "Maybe he went rogue because my dad *is* still in there."

"I don't know, Wyatt," Dru said. "If we could get closer or at least get more footage of him, we might be able to tell."

"He just freezes our damn ships though," Cas said, sighing.

"What about the other facilities on the planet?" Quinn typed away at her tablet. "It looks like there are four private facilities, no cities or towns."

"They, uh, evacuated the planet," Cas said.

"Before he landed? How did they know to do that?" Quinn tapped her fingers on the table, brow furrowed.

"They all left a week after he landed," Cas said. "From what our surveillance shows, they packed absolutely everything. We've reached out, but they won't take our calls."

"Maybe I can try," Wyatt said. "One of the facilities was a medical research lab that worked closely with the GACP. I have a contact there."

"Give it a try now, if you don't mind," Dru said.

Wyatt leaned over and dialed his friend. Moira answered immediately. "Wyatt," she said in surprise, then took in all the faces in the room. "Who are your friends? Can we talk in private? I called the GACP, but they said you didn't work for them anymore."

"Hey, Moira," he said. "These are friends of mine from Charybdis Station. If you don't mind, I'd like them to hear us. I take it you know something about Dad?"

"Baby, that thing isn't your dad anymore," she said. "I don't know what it is, but your dad couldn't have done what that thing did."

"Thing?" Wyatt felt tears prick his eyes. He thought of how they described Water – thing, creature, it, murderous monster.

"The owner of our facility allowed two ships to land at our private port. They were Concord Mercenaries. Your father showed up within an hour of them landing. He... he did something to them. He just walked toward them and then stopped. Some shimmery gas-like substance left each of the mercenaries and went into Dr. Morrick. Seconds later, the mercenaries lay on the ground in comatose states," she said. "I've never seen anything like it."

"He took their souls," Linc whispered, eyes wide. He pulled Nugget close to him.

"I don't know what he did," Moira said. "After that, he turned to me and said that I needed to get all my people off his planet within the week."

"Wait," Cas said. "Did he call you by name? What were his exact words?"

"He said, *Moira, if you want your friends and co-workers to live, leave my planet. I'll give you until the end of the week to pack up and get out. Don't come back.* The owner was right beside me. He didn't even hesitate. He just ordered us to pack up. We put the Concords back on their ship and a couple of volunteers flew them to Union Station for pick-up."

"He said her name," Wyatt said. Hope filled him. His dad *was* still there somewhere.

"Was the owner of your facility friendly with the Concords?" Hazel asked.

"Hell no," Moira said. "He let them land because they paid him, but he had no love for those assholes. We found prisoners on their ships, Wyatt. It was horrible." She nibbled her lip. "My boss had heard of Dr. Morrick though. We've been working on figuring out what happened to him. So far, we think it's some kind of virus."

"Not quite," Wyatt said. "What about the other facilities? Do you know anything about them?"

"Same thing happened at the other two. The Concords paid an exorbitant amount of credits to land, then Dr. Morrick showed up, did his thing, and ordered them off the planet. So far, no one stayed behind. If any ship gets too close to the planet's atmosphere, it freezes. We don't know what kind of technology he's using, but we know it's him," she said. "Wyatt, we're trying to figure out how to help him, but it's not looking good."

"Thank you, Moira," he said. "You have no idea how much that means to me." He sighed. "I *do* know what's going on with him, and I will deal with it. We'll be in touch." Wyatt ended the call and looked at his friends.

"He *is* in there," Dru said. "He knew your friend's name."

"Water wouldn't have hesitated to kill every last one of them," Dru said.

"So," Morgan said, leaning back in his chair. He

laced his fingers with Wyatt's. "Death has gone rogue, and the Concords don't like it. Some of Dr. Morrick is left within him."

"I have an idea why," Dru said. She leaned over and dialed Leti. After a few minutes, Leti's face filled the screen. He looked like he was about to give birth right then, but the poor man still had a month to go.

"Hi guys," he said. "What do you want?"

"Is someone feeling irritable?" Cas tried for a charming grin.

"Fuck off," Leti said. "I want my son out of me. Right now."

"One more month, Leti," Wyatt said. "You can do it."

The gentle man growled. Princess Buttercup stood on his hind legs, his head pressing against Leti's. The Fire Veil dragon hissed at them through the screen. Leti smiled and scratched the scales under his chin. "You're such a good boy," he said.

"Okay. Before Princess tries to eat us through the screen, we have a question for you," Dru said. "Where do the souls of the hosts go during the ritual to bring the Elements into their new bodies?"

"Uh," Leti said, tapping his chin. "I have no idea. Well, I do for Death. He has to draw the soul back into the body for it to work, so I guess the soul would stay there."

Sebastian bent over Leti's shoulder. "For the living hosts, the texts don't mention the souls directly. They do a purifying ritual at the very start to ready the bodies. That may cleanse the bodies of the original inhabitants' souls."

"Death, though, would need the soul to form a connection with the body," Leti said. "Hmm, this just keeps getting more and more interesting." He shook his head. "Why do you ask?"

"Dad is still in there," Wyatt said. "He is Death, but Dad has some control too."

Leti's eyes grew big. "Wyatt..."

Wyatt leaned over and cut off the call. "I'm going to Frost Veil," he said. "I'll take a shuttle. More than likely, Death will just freeze my ship, but I read Dad's letters. Every single one of them. If he will let anyone on the planet, it's me."

"You aren't going alone," Morgan said. "I know you have to do this. We'll send your parents on to Charybdis Station with the kids."

"Cas, do you have a couple of ships we can use," Dru asked. "One to get Wyatt's family home fast and one to take Water's artifact back to the station? It would be best if they travel separately."

"Only if you let me come with you," Cas said.

"Dru," Wyatt said. "You're going to Charybdis Station. Why can't you take Mom and the kids?"

"The Blue Sparrow is going with you, idiot," she said. "Anyone who doesn't want to come can catch a ride with your mom." She looked around the table. Each person met her gaze, faces set.

"Alois," Morgan said. "You need to get back to Sebastian."

"I will," he said. "When the mission is finished. Wyatt is right. We're not done yet."

22

*M*organ hugged Estella one more time. "I don't know why I have to go," she said. "I want to stay with you and Wyatt."

"We want you with us too, sweetie, but we can't put you in danger." He refused to sugarcoat it for her. She had been through too much to be shielded from the truth now.

"He'll need me," she said, eyes imploring. "The monster is his daddy, and he'll have to face it. He'll need me to hold him while he cries."

"I'll hold him," Morgan whispered to her. "I'll hold him until you can. Alright?"

She reluctantly nodded, hugging her stuffed whatever to her chest. Morgan still didn't know what kind of animal it was, but it comforted her. She turned to Wyatt to give him his share of love. Morgan knelt in front of the stroller and checked on Kiki and Pela one more time. It hurt so much to send his three girls away, but it had to be done.

Sandra stood beside him and patted his shoulder. She had aged overnight after watching the recording of Death wearing Morrick's body.

"We'll protect them, Morgan," she said. "Please, protect my Wyatt. If Verion is in there somewhere, I know he won't hurt him, but nothing is certain. Is it?"

"I will guard him with my life," Morgan said, rising to his feet. "We'll try to save Morrick too."

"Wyatt showed me a few of his letters," she said. "I wish I had known. I wish he could have told us what he felt. He was a good man."

"He was," Morgan said, surprised when Sandra hugged him.

"You're a good man too," she said. "I'm glad you're Wyatt's mate." She released him and pushed him into Jordan's arms, then headed for Wyatt.

The kind man hugged him tightly. "Your girls will be fine. We're going to have to fight with Sebastian, Leti, and Ma to keep them until you two get home. They won't lack for love."

"Thank you, Jordan, for everything." Morgan squeezed the man.

"We'll be waiting on you."

Morgan held Wyatt's hand as they watched their family climb aboard the Green Wren. Water's artifact had already left aboard the Green Sparrow that morning. Morgan had to admit he was relieved it wouldn't be traveling with the kids. Now that he knew it existed, he cringed when he thought about how long it had been crammed under their bed.

"Alright," Dru said. "We're resupplied and as ready

as we're ever going to be." She looked over her crew. "You all sure you want to do this? You can still catch a ride on a different ship."

"If we didn't want to be here, we wouldn't be," Linc said. "We're good to go, Captain."

"Rune? You're not a soldier. Are you sure?"

"I'm not leaving Wyatt's side. I told you before. I go where he goes," Rune said.

"Rune," Wyatt said. "This is going to be really dangerous."

"All the more reason for me to go," the big man said. "We're friends, yeah, but this whole thing with your dad could go wrong fast. There will likely be injuries, and you're going to be distracted. I won't be."

"Then you're a fucking member of my crew," Dru said. "I'll add you to the payroll, damn it."

"Finally! You can start having feelings conversations with the new guy," Morgan said.

Dru glared at him.

"It was bound to happen sooner or later," Lerais said. "The man saved Dru's life like six times."

"Four times," Dru said. "Wyatt treated me the other two times."

"Sweet mama, you need to stop getting injured."

"We were taking back a world," she said, hands on her hips. "Every single one of us got badly injured at some point. Even you."

"Excuse me," a man said. He stood beside Morgan's group with a small bag in his hand. He was short and slender, with black eyes and hair. His pointed ears curved against his head. Despite his delicate frame, his features were rough, but maybe that was just the scowl he wore.

"What do you want?" Dru eyed him suspiciously.

She is so good with people, Morgan thought with a smile.

"I'm going with you to Frost Veil," the man said. "Leti called my brother because he was worried about some man named Wyatt. My brother insisted I come help with this idiotic mission of yours."

Morgan had Leti on his comm before the man finished. "Leti, who's this guy?"

"Oh, that's Beol. He's the Guild Master of the Half-Moon Assassins. Hi, Beol!" Leti's little holographic figure waved at Beol. "He's my friend Wolfe's brother. Beol, you could have sent one of your people. I really appreciate your help, but I know you're busy with the move."

"Like I'd send one of my people on this fool's errand. I read your report and watched your presentation. Plus, my guys told me what happened on Tammol. It would be easier to just blast the shit out of the man's lab from the sky." His scowl deepened. "Fucking dead people walking around alive is some messed-up shit."

"Uh, welcome aboard," Dru said, shrugging.

Silverlight System, Planet Frost Veil

"Okay," Linc said. "This is really weird." The Blue Sparrow eased past the frozen Charybdis Station ships. "How long does he keep them frozen?"

"About fifteen minutes," Cas said. "We're already in the planet's atmosphere. Holy shit. None of my ships have gotten this far."

"Do you think it's because I'm on board?" Wyatt sat in a corner chair with Luna. He hugged the furry dog tightly. Morgan stood beside him, holding one of his hands. Morgan wasn't sure how he felt about the hope flaring in his husband's eyes. On one hand, he wanted Morrick to still be present. On the other hand, they seldom got what they wanted. He thought of Kiki and Pela's sacrifice.

"I don't know, Wyatt," Cas said. "It makes more sense than anything else does. Don't get your hopes up too high. Okay?"

"I'm a practical person, Cas," Wyatt said.

Morgan nodded. His husband was practical in some ways. He was also a goofy, soft-hearted romantic.

"Where do you want to land, Captain?" Nugget stretched along the back of Linc's chair.

Morgan still didn't like the cat, but her presence made Linc happier and less nervous. Nugget looked at him and hissed. Fucking cat was worse than Leti's dragon. He really needed his own pet.

"Any signs of other ships?" Dru sat in the captain's chair, back straight. If she was nervous or afraid, it didn't show. The whole situation with Tammol had allowed her to come into her own. Morgan felt a burst of pride. He knew he would follow her anywhere, even if she had made him have a *talk* with her when they landed on Union Station.

"Uh, yeah." Linc double-checked his readings. "There are two small ships in the private spaceport closest to Morrick's former lab. My scan shows several people gathered around the space port. No other groups though."

"Why aren't they frozen in space like the others?"

"Think about it," Beol said. "Who might be a match for the power of Death?"

"Life," Wyatt said. "Why would he come here?"

"If Death did go rogue, it makes sense that the Queen would send someone to collect him," Dru said. "Who would be better at that than Life?"

"Where should I land?" Linc asked.

"Shit. We don't want to be seen by the ships down there, but we need to be close to the lab," Dru said.

Beol sighed and stood. "I'll go speak with your engineer. You can have one of our cloaking devices."

Dru watched him go. "That guy seriously grates on my nerves."

"Is it because the two of you are kind of alike? You're both grumpy, rude, blunt, and growly," Wyatt said.

"Why do I like you?" Dru glared at Morgan's husband.

The ship shuddered.

"What was that?" Linc asked.

"That would be the cloaking device," Beol said, sitting back in his chair. "It physically hides the ship and prevents us from being scanned. Land, so we can get this shit over with."

"I guess you're useful." Dru shrugged. "Land between the lab and the spaceport. We'll scout out the spaceport first. See who's there."

"Sure thing, Captain," Linc said and brought the ship down in the snow. "My scans show those ships are Concord ships."

"Morgan, you and I will go and see what we can see," Dru said.

"A storm is on the way," Linc said. "You have maybe two hours before it hits."

"I'll come with," Beol said. "I have personal cloaking shields too." He reluctantly handed each person in the room a shield. "Make sure I get all of this back when we finish. Assuming we're alive."

"Definitely grating on my nerves," Dru mumbled. "Dress warm and meet me at the door in fifteen minutes."

Morgan and Wyatt went back to their room, and Morgan hurriedly dressed in his heated gear. He quickly braided his long hair and grabbed his ski mask. Wyatt cupped his face, leaning up to press a kiss to his lips.

"Be careful, baby. I love you," Wyatt said.

"I'll be back before you know it, kitten."

Wyatt rushed to his medical bag. He pulled out familiar looking injectors. "I'll give everyone a couple of them, but here." He handed him six.

"I'll give some to Dru and Beol too." He got one more kiss, then they separated in the hall. Wyatt headed for the bridge, and Morgan headed for the door at the back of the ship.

"Here are injectors of the poison that killed Water," Morgan said, handing them to Beol and Dru.

"I really hope we don't have to use these," Dru said.

"I have something else though," Beol said, smirking.

"Could you not have led with that, asshole?" Dru moved toward the closest wall.

"Nope," Beol said. "How thick do you think it is?"

"Two feet," she said. "I remember checking it when we were here the first time. We needed to either go through the gates or the wall. The gates were only a foot thick." She deactivated her shield. "Give me whatever you have, Beol." He drew his Vibro-sword and handed it to her. "That's it?"

He pushed a button on the end and molten fire spread through the blade. "There. The walls are mostly ice. This will work."

"Thank fuck for environmentally concerned scientists," Morgan said.

Dru made quick work of cutting a short door in the wall. Beol finished cutting the chains and politely held out his hand for his sword. "I believe that's mine."

"I want it," Dru said, pouting.

"Keep wanting," Beol said.

She threw it at him and stomped through the door. "Linc," Dru called him through the comm.

"Captain?"

"Give me ten minutes, then move the ship behind the back wall of the spaceport. I'll send you the exact coordinates."

"Yes, sir."

"Let's take out some patrols, guys," Dru said.

Beol drew his swords. "Finally."

Dru stared at the shiny, flaming blades, pining.

He paused. "Ugh. Here." He handed Dru one of his weapons.

She wiggled with happiness and took it. "You're the best."

Morgan rolled his eyes, then turned to the prisoners. "Stay here while we clear the way. We'll be right back." They looked around, and he realized they couldn't see him. That was so awesome. "Beol, I'm keeping the shield. Just so you know."

The man growled.

There were only six guards along the wall, and they were quickly dispatched in the dark. Morgan heard the slight impact as the ship landed and headed back to the prisoners. He deactivated his shield. "Come on," he said. "Let's get you all aboard."

They followed him through the hole in the wall, then looked around. "It's this way," Beol said, appearing suddenly. He patted the ship. "The door is to the left of me." The prisoners walked forward slowly, each disappearing inside. Morgan followed behind them.

Wyatt grabbed him in a hug, then let him go to start leading the prisoners to the med-bay. "Come on, folks. Rune and I will take care of your injuries, then get you some food to warm you up."

Dru appeared beside him. "Everyone's onboard, Linc. Get us out of here."

The ship lifted off, and they flew closer to the lab.

"Did you find anything?" Quinn asked. She and Hazel waited with Linc on the bridge.

"Just prisoners and a cute little dragon," Morgan said. He pulled the tiny thing out of his pocket. It curled into his palm and blinked its huge blue eyes at him. Luna looked up at him, so he knelt so she could sniff the dragon. She licked its head, then went off in search of Wyatt.

"Fuck me," Dru said. "We *do not* need another dragon."

"They were roasting its mom, Dru," Morgan said. "I couldn't just leave it behind."

Linc's eyes were big. "You found your pet, Morgan."

"I never should have told you about that," he muttered.

"Anyway," Dru said, eyeing his dragon. "Life wasn't there."

"Do you think he's at the lab?" Hazel asked.

"Nowhere else to be, unless he's walking around the cold, empty wasteland," Quinn said.

"Get some rest," Dru said. "The storm is moving through. We'll see what we can find out in the morning."

Morgan shucked his heavy clothes in his room and dressed in his normal uniform. He found Luna sitting outside the med-bay. She wagged her tail when she saw him and sniffed his pocket.

"Such a smart girl," he said, petting her ears. "I put the baby back in my pocket. Did Wyatt kick you out?"

"The doctor said it was too crowded in there," a girl said. She was young, maybe seventeen at the most.

"Thank you," Morgan said. "She's a people dog, poor girl." He tried to pet Luna's head, puzzled when she ducked behind him, growling.

"Were you guys looking for their leader? He's really creepy," the girl said.

"Yeah. We were hoping to isolate him from the others," Morgan said. "Do you know where he went?"

"I heard them say he was going to a lab to get his brother."

"Brother, huh? That's not good."

"They said the Queen was really angry. Are there even queens left in the galaxy?" The girl frowned.

"There are a few," Morgan said. "This queen, though, isn't like the others."

"They whisper about her."

"What do they say?"

"They say she is the most powerful being in the galaxy and all will bow down to her," the girl said. "They were going to bring us to serve her." She shuddered. "Thank you for bringing us in from the cold."

"My pleasure, kid," Morgan said. "Hey. Look at what I found in their camp." He reached in and pulled out the little dragon. The baby took one look at the girl and hissed, glaring at her.

The girl snarled. "Filthy beast," she said, getting to her feet.

"Don't call it that," Morgan said, confused.

The girl looked at him with hate-filled eyes. "We were meant to serve the Queen." She lunged for him, fingers curved.

Suddenly, Beol was there, holding her back.

"Life must have gotten to her," Morgan said. "Fuck. Dru, help us," he called into his comm.

"Morgan!" Wyatt's cry filled him with fear. Luna ran into the room, barking and growling. He stashed the little hissing beastie in his pocket and ran to his mate.

Three of the prisoners were attacking the others. Rune held one, and Wyatt stood in front of a group of the youngest prisoners, facing the other two. Luna growled and jumped on one, bringing the man to the ground. A couple of the other prisoners grabbed the fallen man's arms, holding him down. Wyatt punched the last one, knocking him back into Morgan's arms.

Dru and the others ran in, looking around.

"What the hell?" Quinn exclaimed.

"Life must have influenced some of them," Morgan said, holding the squirming man.

Dru adjusted her phaser and tranquilized the two men and one woman. They fell to the ground unconscious. "Beol has the girl. Quinn and Hazel, lock them up." She looked around. "How can we tell that was all?"

"Maybe I can," Morgan said. "Come on Luna," he said and pulled the little dragon out of his pocket again. It looked grumpy. "Sorry, buddy. I'll let you rest in just a minute." They walked around the room, and Luna only barked at one more person. The little dragon hissed at the same time.

The woman they pointed out watched them coldly. "The Queen will peel the skin from your body."

"Yeah, yeah." Dru tranquilized her. "I'll put her with the others." She tossed the woman over her shoulder and headed out the door.

"Morgan?" Wyatt looked at the little dragon.

"Hey, kitten," Morgan said. "Are you okay? Was anyone hurt?"

"No. Rune reacted fast, and you were right there." He pointed at the dragon. "What is that?"

"You said that one day I'd meet my pet. That I would just know," he said and fluttered his eyes. "I love you, kitten."

Beol snorted from behind him. Morgan ignored him.

"Is that a dragon like Princess?" Wyatt looked horrified.

"I think so. It's just a baby." He held it up. "You wouldn't want me to abandon a baby, would you?" The little dragon cooed, batting its eyes.

"Oh gods. It's you in dragon form," Alois said from beside him.

"It is definitely counting as one of our eight kids," Wyatt said, stroking a finger over its tiny head.

24

*W*yatt watched Morgan sleep, a sliver of moonlight falling across his face. The little dragon, a boy they'd discovered, lay on his husband's pillow, curled up and purring. Little puffs of icy air hit Morgan's face with each of the dragon's breaths.

Luna watched him from the foot of the bed. Wyatt reached down and ran his hands through her fur, pressing his face to her side.

"I can't risk them, Luna," he whispered.

Quietly, he pulled on the heavy, heated clothes that Morgan had left in piles on the floor. He patted his pocket, assured the injectors were still there. Luna followed him from the room.

"No. You have to stay here, Luna. It's too cold outside for doggies."

His dog didn't seem to care. She tilted her head, then gave a light bark.

"No. Shush, girl." He met her stubborn eyes. "You are horrible."

He went back in their room and dug around for one of her sweaters. Morgan's snores stuttered, and Wyatt's eyes flew to his husband. Still asleep. He made it back out the door and sneaked down the hall.

Rune was looking after the prisoners in the med-bay. They were mostly suffering from malnourishment and frostbite. He snuck to the door of the ship and eased it open. The lab wasn't even a mile away. He could get there, look for his dad, then come back before anyone woke up. He left the ship and started walking.

"The lab is the other way," Beol said from beside him.

Wyatt squealed and jumped. Luna licked the man's gloved hand, saying hello.

"What are you doing?" Wyatt asked.

"Following you to make sure you don't die."

"How did you know I came out here?"

"You weren't exactly quiet. Your husband must sleep like the dead."

"My husband is perfect," Wyatt said hotly.

"Okay," Beol said. "I won't point out facts about your husband."

He walked beside him in silence.

"Why aren't you trying to stop me?" Wyatt finally asked.

"One, I couldn't stop you unless I knocked you unconscious. Two, you're Death's weakness. We need to see how that will work."

"I'll kill him if I have to," Wyatt said. "Do you still have your injectors?"

"Yes," Beol said. "I'm sorry, Wyatt. It's a hard thing you have to do."

"It is," he agreed softly. "Maybe I won't. Maybe he'll still be in there."

"I hope so."

"Wolfe is your brother?"

"Yes. I love him very much."

Wyatt didn't know why he was so surprised the man had a soft spot. Everyone did.

"I've talked to him a few times. I know sign language, so he calls when he gets bored," Wyatt said. He laughed. "He tells the dumbest jokes."

"He really does," Beol said.

The lab was quiet and dark. The door stood open, snow blowing into the entry.

"I guess we're doing this," Wyatt whispered.

The first room made Wyatt gag. It was full of the bodies of the scientists and security guards of the facility.

It looked as though Death had taken their souls and piled them in there to waste away. At least the room was ice cold so the stench was minimal. It also looked like some wildlife had taken to munching on the buffet.

"This isn't a good start," Beol said.

"Let's keep going," Wyatt said, covering his mouth. They walked on. The next few rooms were empty. There was a large staff kitchen. Someone had recently eaten cereal. The dirty dishes stood in the sink. "Maybe you should wait here."

"No. If Life is in there too, you'll need me."

"He's not here." Verion Morrick stood in the middle of the next room, a sitting room full of couches and chairs. His pale white skin was covered by more than a sheet now. He still didn't wear shoes though, just black pants and a thin, grey shirt.

"Dad?"

"Wyatt, you shouldn't have come." His eyes were black, but his face belonged to Verion Morrick.

Wyatt sobbed and ran to him.

His dad wrapped his cold arms around him, resting his face in Wyatt's hair. "My boy. How I've missed you."

"You said, *I love you more than all the stardust in the galaxy.* Remember?"

"I do," Verion said. "I love you so much, son."

"I love you too, Dad. I'm sorry I was such a jerk when we talked last time. I didn't know you loved me," Wyatt said. "I do now."

"Sir," Beol said. "I'm sorry to interrupt, but you said that Life isn't here?"

"He went back to check on his men." Verion grinned. "It seems someone attacked them." His grin faded. "Life," he said. "Death, Air, Water, Fire, and Earth. They are good translations of our names, but I know this new time finds it strange to be named such things."

"Death? You are Death then?" Wyatt leaned back, looking at his dad's dark, unfamiliar eyes.

"Yes. I am Death, and I am Verion Morrick. We are one and the same. It was the strangest thing. As soon as my soul settled into my body again, we merged and became one person."

"So you aren't going to fight for the Queen? You'll come home with me?" Wyatt said.

"It's not that easy, son," Verion said. "If I fight for her, she will spare you. If I don't, they'll do their best to kill you. That's why Life is here – to bring me back to her."

"You can't," Wyatt said. "She's evil. Water served her, and he killed millions of people before we killed him."

Verion looked at him in shock. "You killed him?"

"Yes," Wyatt said. "I'll find a way to kill him in his container too. I just haven't had the chance."

"Son, that is… I'm proud of you." He hugged Wyatt again. "I know that's not something I should be proud of, but Water was an evil bastard. All of them are really, except one."

"Come on," Wyatt said, tugging on his dad's arm. "Let's go."

Luna growled deep, and Beol activated his shield, disappearing.

"Yes, brother. Why don't you go with him?" Life strolled into the room. He wore a Concord uniform, but he looked odd in it.

He was Silet. That was it. An obvious, glittery-skinned non-human wore a Concord uniform. Odd. His eyes were the coldest, cruelest things Wyatt had ever seen. He stepped between his father and Life.

"Leave him be," Verion said. "We've made no agreements yet. I'll serve the Queen."

"Yes, you will," Life said. "Maybe, your host's son

will too, hmm? I swear you have the worst luck with hosts. It must be those pesky souls you require."

He looked at Wyatt and smiled. Suddenly, the Silet looked like a kind, charming man. The crinkles at the corners of his eyes reminded Wyatt of Jordan.

He held his arms out. "Come here, dear. I know there's something I can give you. Something you want."

Wyatt's heart melted. He smiled and ran to him, eager for a warm hug. It was so cold. The galaxy was such a scary place, and he wanted to feel safe. He wanted his family and friends to be safe too.

Luna barked, deep and quick. He looked back. She stood beside Verion, watching Wyatt.

"There is something, I want," Wyatt said, looking back at the smiling man. "I know you can give it to me. I just know it."

"Wyatt, no. Don't let him in." Verion's voice was so sad. "You don't know what he'll do, and I have no power against him. I can't even move."

"You poor boy." Life waved his arms. "Come on. Yes, dearest. Anything you want." The man's black eyes sparkled with joy and happiness.

Wyatt stepped into his embrace, sighing.

"I want Kiki and Pela back," he said, voice shaking. "I want the Tammolians to be okay. I want my father to be safe." He pressed the injector into Life's back. "I want you and your fucking queen to die."

As the last word left his mouth, Wyatt was ripped out of Life's arms, Beol's grip on his shoulders tight. He found himself back beside his father.

Verion wrapped him in his arms, shaking.

"What did you do?" Life shook and whined. "I don't feel good. What did you do?"

"He's Silet," Wyatt said. "Shit." He didn't know how the poison would react to the different race.

"On it." Beol's voice came from beside him. Seconds later, two more injectors jabbed into Life. Then it was done.

Wyatt closed his eyes, glad he was far enough away from the man to miss the splatter. Beol deactivated his shield and stood from behind a large chair.

"That's really messy," he said. "Damn, Wyatt."

"Get his artifact," Verion said, nodding toward a small pyramid lying in a pile of body bits.

"I don't want to touch it," Beol said.

"I don't either," Verion said. "You're closer."

"Oh for the love of…" Wyatt tiptoed through the mess and picked up the artifact. Somehow, it was still clean.

"I'll fight beside you, son," Verion said. "Life was the Queen's lover and the man she trusted to keep the rest of us in check. He was the only one who could control me. I *will* fight beside you."

"Hmm," Beol said. "You just don't want to get stuck with one of those injectors."

Verion grinned. "That's a benefit too, yes." He froze, eyes vague. "It looks like the Concords are freaking out. Some of them must have been under his influence. They're attacking your ship. Why are they attacking your ship bare-handed? Idiots."

His black eyes changed. It looked like they filled with grey and white clouds, swirling together. Shiny, grey wisps flew into the room. They came straight through the walls and into Verion. After a moment, they stopped. "There. That should make your friends happy."

"Thank you, Luna. I almost fell for Life's act," Wyatt said, bending to hug Luna. "Oh, yeah, Dad. I got married, and I have an adopted daughter and twins."

Verion looked shocked. "It's been less than a year."

Wyatt shrugged. "Things happen." His comm started beeping. "Uh oh. Morgan is going to be pissed."

"Morgan? The Charybdis Station mercenary with the shiny hair?"

Wyatt smiled. "That's my mate and husband."

"We're okay, pretty boy." Beol spoke into his comm. "I know you were concerned about me too."

"Where are you?" Morgan's voice was strained.

"In the lab. Wyatt and I killed Life, and Death slash Verion is a good guy."

"We're on our way. Tell my husband he is in big trouble."

Beol looked at him. "You're in big trouble."

25

*M*organ ran straight to Wyatt. "Kitten, I am so mad at you. Why didn't you wait for us?" He pulled him into a hug, even as he kept muttering. His body shook against Wyatt's.

"While I wish my son had never put himself in danger, I must admit that he and Beol handled this better than your team could have. Life didn't see him as a threat, and he didn't see Beol at all," Verion said.

"Well, that's gross," Dru said, wrinkling her nose at the sight of Life's remains. "At least that's done." She turned to Verion. "So, you're a good guy?"

"I will be for Wyatt," Verion said.

"You said all but one of the Elements is completely evil," Wyatt said. "You weren't talking about yourself, were you?"

"No. Until my last host, I was just like them. I served the Queen faithfully."

"Okay," Cas said. "We need to hear this, but we don't need to hear it here. Let's get back on the ship and head home. We'll call the others. Dr. Morrick, I imagine you don't want to have to repeat your story a hundred times."

"I would rather not." He looked around. "I suppose my planet will be alright in my absence."

"Your planet?" Quinn tried to hide a smile. "You can't just take a planet."

Verion arched a brow. "Yet here we are. This planet suits me and keeps me away from others. That's better for everyone."

They walked through the front room.

"When this is over, we need to spruce it up a bit, Dad. You really don't need dead bodies lying around your home," Wyatt said.

"As you wish, son."

"Spoiled," Hazel coughed into her hand. She cleared her throat and smiled innocently.

The ship was parked right outside the lab, and the morning sun glistened off the blue metal. Wyatt supposed there wasn't much reason to hide anymore. All the Concords on the planet were dead. Linc and Lerais met them at the door.

"Dru, I do not like being left behind," Lerais said.

"You're the engineer, honey. It's going to happen. It never made Beck happy either," Dru said. "How are the corrupted prisoners?"

"Crazy," Linc said, following them all to the conference room. "We had to tie them down. They were hurting themselves."

"Life's victims never were able to survive without him," Verion said sadly.

"I'll get us in the air," Linc said. He hugged Wyatt, surprising him. "I'm glad you're safe, Wyatt. Morgan was really worried."

Wyatt looked at Morgan. His husband was glaring at him. "I'm sorry. I didn't want to risk any more lives for my own softheartedness."

"Why did Beol get to go?" Morgan actually sounded jealous.

"Because he's a stalkery weirdo," Wyatt said. Morgan looked at least a little appeased.

"I'm glad I could be there for you, Wyatt," Beol said dryly.

They piled in the conference room. On the vidscreen, Leti rubbed the sleep from his eyes and looked at everyone. "Give me an hour. I'll get everyone together and call you back." He smiled tremulously toward Verion, then glared at Wyatt. "I'm not happy with you. You hung up on me last time." He sniffed.

"You sent Beol after me," Wyatt said. "We're even."

"I'm sitting right next to you," Beol said, rolling his eyes.

"One hour."

An hour later, the entire council and all of Blue Solace were gathered. The Lord Admiral stared hard at Wyatt's dad. "Dr. Morrick? Is it truly you?"

"Mostly," Verion said. "I guess that's as good a place to start as any. I'm both Verion Morrick and the being you call Death. We are completely merged. Both of our personalities and memories are present. We have one will and one mind. During the ritual, assuming it goes right, my host's soul is pulled back into my body, and

C.W. GRAY

we merge. That's why it's so important that the host be willing."

"Are the others different?" Wyatt didn't recognize the council member who asked the question.

"Yes," Verion said. "My Queen is typically summoned first. She takes any present body she chooses. Then she raises her Elements. Their hosts are purged of their souls, and the Elements take over. I am always raised last since it is more involved."

"Why aren't you heading straight for your queen?" Renee Juren asked. The station's head of security looked delicate and sweet, but Morgan assured Wyatt that she was a force of her own. She stood beside her husband, Fasi, to serve the station, and there was nothing passive about her.

Verion's black eyes filled with sadness. "Let me start at the beginning. Millennia ago, long before the Crells developed space travel, my Queen was a normal Crellic woman on Genarg. War ravaged the world and her whole family was killed. She vowed she would bring peace to the world, no matter what she had to do. She began studying with the Crellic Shamans. In those times, they were beyond powerful. The Queen grew to be the most powerful of them all and bound the six Elements to her. She provided us with our first host bodies, and we served her completely. With our help, she ruled the world and brought peace to her people."

"This all sounds a little too clean-cut," Leti said. "Were her intentions really good?"

"That first time, yes," he answered. "She kept Life, Air, and Water's more violent tendencies controlled.

Earth worshiped her, but he always has. Fire and I were left to our own devices when we weren't needed. We all passed naturally that cycle, our essences moving to our containers when we died. It was a bare but beautiful life."

"When did it change?" Sebastian asked.

"The next cycle," Verion answered. "The Crells were fighting again, tearing the planet apart. They remembered my Queen, though, and the peace she maintained. The Shamans created the ritual to resurrect her. They weren't as good as their ancestors, and she came back, but she wasn't the woman she had been. We are bound to her, so we all felt it. She changed and forced us to change with her. That cycle and all the hundreds of others were the same. We didn't bring peace. We brought death and ruin. She wasn't the kind and intelligent woman she had been. She reveled in spilling the blood of others. That second cycle was when she and Life became inseparable. I think it's the utter control he has over his victims that attracted her to him. She holds that same control over us."

"Life is dead now," Dru said and reviewed the events of the past few hours for their audience.

"She won't be happy about that," Hack said.

"No." Verion's smile was bitter but pleased. "She won't."

"What changed you?" Fasi asked. "You obviously aren't following her anymore."

Verion's smile disappeared. "There have been times when one or more of the Elements have rebelled, wanting to go their own way. My Queen is quick to rein us back in. Air and Water both like the killing and would sometimes kill too many, too fast. Life and I were the ones sent to bring them back." His eyes softened. "Fire runs every cycle. He's hates the violence. Funny, isn't it? By nature, he is destructive, but in reality, the man is a soft-hearted, free spirit. My Queen binds him several times a cycle to keep him in her control."

"That explains why he's the only one always pictured wearing a collar," Leti said. He looked at Verion, considering. "During the last cycle, *you* rebelled. Didn't you? You're the enforcer, but you wanted out. That's why you're not in the pictures."

"My host was different than the others that time. He was happily married, but he was also mated to his wife. He chose to be a sacrifice, because he wanted to protect her and his people. After we merged, those feelings were still there. I'd never felt anything like it, not really. In the past, I stayed cold and isolated. It was strange. He still loved her, so I loved her. It was awkward at first, but she came to love the new me. We were happy."

"In the histories, Leti said that the Queen is summoned to help people, but it's not long before that changes, and she ruins everything," a councilwoman said. "I'm guessing the woman you loved didn't like that change."

"No," Verion said. "When it became clear my Queen would ruin the Crells, my wife and I gathered as many as we could and fled to the farthest planet in the Crellic System."

"Dargner," Hack said.

"Yes. She sent Air, Water, and Fire after me. I killed them all, even poor Fire," he said. "Then she came. She had never left Genarg before. They all came. I killed Earth, but the Queen and Life killed me. I don't know what happened after that."

"From what I can tell, the last of the Crells were able to put her back to sleep," Leti said. "That explains why the Belcorts found you all there."

"When I merged with my host this time, it was like before. I love Wyatt very much," Verion said. "I'll do anything to protect my son, even if it means killing my Queen." He shook his head. "She isn't my Queen anymore."

"Water and Life are both dead," Sebastian said. "You're out of her reach. Will she stop?"

"No," Leti said, shaking his head. "It's not in her nature to stop."

"He's right," Verion said. "Likely, she will send Fire and Air after me."

"Fire," Sebastian said, tapping his chin. "I'll start looking at the bindings on his collar. I wonder if we could free him. What would he do?"

Verion snorted. "He'd eat you out of house and home, then find a nice, hot planet to run around on."

"Would he join us in fighting the Queen?" Renee asked.

"I don't know," Verion said, shrugging. "He wouldn't fight for her. That's all I'm sure of."

"Possibilities," Leti said, musing. "We know more now. The Queen is down three of her six elements. Wolfe and his team are starting to send in information from their end." He nodded to Wyatt. "We have a way to kill them."

"Come home," Fasi said, standing suddenly. "Come home and we'll plan. Cas, focus on the Concords in the Silverlight System. Without Life to lead them, they should be scattering right now. Beol?"

"You're going to give me a mission, aren't you?" Beol watched the screen warily. "You know I'm not one of your generals."

"Not yet," Fasi said with a grin. "Will you check with your contacts? Water decimated a world. I wonder what Air and Fire have been up to. Please see if you can find anything out."

"Fucking mission. I knew it," Beol muttered.

Silverlight System, Planet Union Station

WYATT ENJOYED Cas's bear hug. "You behave, Wyatt. I'll see you back at Charybdis Station one day," the large blue Grell said. "Take care of pretty boy here."

"I will," Wyatt said. "Be careful. I think the Concords may surprise us yet. Oh, I'll miss your hugs." Back on his feet, he turned to Beol. "We're friends now, Beol," Wyatt said. He held his hand up. "No. No arguing. Leti gets Wolfe, but I get you. Deal with it."

"Why does everyone think I need friends?" Beol distinctly resembled Nugget at his most hissy.

Morgan patted him on the back. "It'll be okay, little buddy." The baby Frost Veil Dragon sat on Morgan's shoulder, reminding Wyatt of Monty.

"*Little?*"

"You're whining, Beol," Wyatt said. "Now, give me a hug. You'll be in Charybdis Station soon enough, and I'll introduce you to my girls." Wyatt pulled the small man into his arms, squeezing him tightly. "Thank you for helping me," he whispered.

Beol just sighed and awkwardly hugged him back. "I'll see you in Charybdis Station." He looked at Morgan. "Oh, and tell Dru her contract is complete."

"Got it," Morgan said, nodding. Together they watched Beol and Cas leave the ship. Morgan turned to Wyatt and cupped his husband's face in his hands, stroking a thumb across Wyatt's lips. "Promise me that you won't leave me behind again."

"Morgan, I didn't leave you behind because I wanted to," Wyatt said. He'd tried to explain a hundred times, but his husband wasn't getting it. "I couldn't let you get hurt just because I wanted my dad."

"Promise me, Wyatt. I'd rather die beside you than be left behind to live."

"Morgan." Wyatt gave up. He was used to being left behind because he was a doctor. Wyatt knew he didn't have to understand it though. He just had to accept it. "Okay. I promise."

Morgan kissed him. "I'd rather you never put yourself in danger at all."

"Don't push your luck."

"Come on. Let's go check on your dad," Morgan

said, grinning. They held hands as they walked down the hall to the bridge. "Did Sebastian steal the girls yet?"

"They just got there this morning," Wyatt said, trying to defend his friend.

"So? Did he?"

"He stole Estella. Your sister stole the twins."

"Really? I can see Selene doing that. I'm surprised Ma didn't get them," Morgan said.

"It's my understanding that they'll be alternating custody," Wyatt said wryly.

Morgan just laughed, his brown eyes sparkling.

"Hey, Dad," Wyatt said. "Do you know anything about Frost Veil Dragons?"

Verion looked up, smiling warmly. He sat in a corner seat, across from Lerais. The two men had spent a lot of time together on the flight from Frost Veil to Union Station. It was weird, but Wyatt had just become *friends* with an Assassin Guild Master.

Luna sat on his feet chewing on one of her toys.

"Not much, really. They're reclusive. I know they eat just about anything and can live for over a hundred years. They're like Fire Veil Dragons in a lot of ways."

"There's not much written about them," Morgan said. "He eats the nasty instant dinners I feed him."

He petted the little dragon's head.

"What did you name him?" Lerais asked.

"I can't decide. I thought of Snowflake or Snowball."

"Those sound like cat names," Wyatt said.

"Whitey?"

"No," Lerais said, shaking his head. "That's just... no."

Verion considered the little dragon. "It doesn't have to be a snow-related name." He looked at Wyatt. "What about Stardust?"

Wyatt's lip trembled, and Morgan's eyes lit up. "Yes! That. It's perfect. We have Stardust and Luna."

Wyatt ignored his husband and wrapped his arms around his dad, shoving himself into his seat. "I love you more than all the stardust in the galaxy, Dad."

26

ANCHOR'S REST SYSTEM, CHARYBDIS
STATION

*M*organ watched Wyatt as they approached Charybdis Station.

"This place is beautiful, Morgan. How is it even possible? I must have been spending way too much time on low-technology planets," Wyatt said.

"I remember the first time I saw it," Morgan said. "I was used to the dirt and grime of the lower city on Union Station. It seemed like heaven." He remembered Ma and Pops meeting them at the gate. They took in all the strays, loving each and every one of them.

"It sure is a pretty place," Rune said. Morgan shot the large man a grin. "Where's Stardust?"

"He's sleeping in my pocket," Morgan said. "I didn't want him to be overwhelmed by all the people. He'll meet his sisters tonight."

"Oh, what a mission," Dru said, rolling her shoulders. "Remember when we left? We thought it would take a month, maybe a month and a half."

"That's the joy of being a captain, Dru," Lerais said.

"You get to see the job through."

"It does feel good," she said. "Well, Morrick, what do you think of the station?"

"Which Morrick?" Morgan asked, knowing full well she meant Verion. "There are three of us here." He had happily taken his husband's name.

"Shut up, pretty boy." She looked at Verion. "Well, Verion?"

Verion looked as awed as Wyatt. "I've never seen anything like it."

"Dr. Manning is looking forward to seeing you," Dru said. "The Lord Admiral told me she wouldn't shut up about it."

"It'll be nice to finally meet Orsla," Verion said.

"You've never met?" Morgan asked.

"Oh, no. I seldom left Frost Veil. We've talked quite a bit though."

"And... we've landed," Alois said. "Finally."

Morgan shot his friend a look. "Why are you so nervous? You're fucking shaking."

Wyatt squealed, startling everyone, Luna included. He clapped his hands. "Sebastian will be there."

Morgan grinned. "You going to kiss him?"

"That would be too presumptuous, wouldn't it?" Alois vibrated in place, eyes full of longing.

"Maybe play it by ear," Wyatt said, trying to hold in a grin. "See how Sebastian reacts."

There was a suspicious twinkle in his eye. Hmm. Wyatt knew how Sebastian would react. Damn those morning talks.

Alois ran to the door, and the others rushed after

him. No one wanted to miss anything. They left the ship and were greeted by a crowd of friends and family. The Lord Admiral and his wife waved from the back. Fasi looked relieved they had finally landed. The rest of Blue Solace were there, along with Ma and Pops and all their kids.

Sebastian ran from the crowd, meeting Alois halfway. The small man pulled Alois's head down and pressed their lips together. Then they were plastered together, bodies entwining, while their kiss deepened.

"I guess they're mates," Quinn said. "Or at least they *really* like each other."

Their kiss ended, and Alois tossed Sebastian over his shoulder. "Love you guys, but see you later," he yelled, running past the crowd.

Sebastian looked up, searching for Wyatt. He waved at Morgan's mate. "Talk to you later, Wyatt. Your kids are great."

Then they were gone. Everyone watched the gate for a minute, blinking.

"They are definitely mates," Wyatt said, breaking the silence. Estella laughed as she threw herself into Wyatt's arms. "Oh, I missed you, sweet girl," he said, hugging her.

"I love you," she said, pressing a kiss to Wyatt's cheek. He set her down, and she rushed to hug Morgan too. He picked her up, laughing at her giggles. "I missed you too, Morgan."

"Good," he said. "No replacing us while we're gone."

"Ma and Pops *are* a lot of fun," she said, shrugging.

"We didn't steal your girl, baby," Ma said, pulling

Morgan, Estella, and Wyatt all into her arms. "Oh, we're glad you're home. Our grandbabies are beautiful, but they need their daddies. Wyatt, your mama is a sweetheart too." She finally released them to Pops, so she could grab an unsuspecting Rune. "Aren't you a sweet boy? Come here and give me some love."

"Welcome home, son," Pops said, hugging them. "Don't let Ma lie to you. She wants those babies. All three."

"I had to fight her for them," Sandra said, pushing through. "Hey, boys." She kissed Wyatt and Morgan both on the cheek. "Where's your father?"

"Right here, Sandra," Verion said.

Sandra turned around and covered her mouth, stifling her sob. She ran to Verion and hugged him. Then she smacked his arm. "Don't you dare die again, Verion. It was horrible."

"I'm sorry?" Verion looked puzzled. She smacked him again, tears streaming down her face.

"Don't try to make sense of it. Just tell her you won't die again," Jordan said, walking up to hold his crying wife.

"I won't die again, Sandra." Verion shot Jordan a thankful look.

"Good," she said, sniffling. She wiped her eyes. "I missed you. No more holding shit in, Verion. We love you. Even Jordan, and he hated you for a long time."

"It's true," Jordan said, nodding affably.

"You don't hate me now? After all I did to Sandra and Wyatt?"

"Oh lord, no. Hating people is way too much effort,"

Jordan said. "Besides, I have Sandra and you don't." He grinned. "That makes me feel better."

Verion gave a startled laugh.

"Verion?" Leti shuffled from foot to foot. His pregnant belly was huge. A small, travel-sized Princess Buttercup rode on his shoulder.

"Leti," Verion said, affection filling his voice. "I'm so glad you're doing well." They hugged.

"I was so mad when you died," Leti said. "You hadn't gotten to see Wyatt again like you wanted."

"Wyatt and I are good now. We're going to make it work," Verion said, wiping Leti's tears from his cheeks. "Leti, thank you for caring about me. Your big heart saved my son, and I will never be able to thank you enough."

"You just called my heart fat, didn't you? So rude," Leti said. Verion laughed, and Leti wiped his face and headed for Wyatt.

The two men hugged for so long that the rest of the group moved around them. Shae brought the twins over so Morgan could coo over them. "Thanks for helping out so much, Shae."

"That's what family is for," the young Siren said. "I'll keep an eye on them while you get your hugs finished. Then you can change Pela's stinky diaper."

"Gee, thanks," Morgan said. He ruffled the man's hair, enjoying the gasp of rage it caused. He talked with Hack and the rest of the crew, hugged Selene, Draif, and Lucas, then got down to changing a stinky diaper.

He did notice something strange. Rune kept fussing over Silas. Leti's guard was still seriously injured, though he was finally getting around. He hated people fussing over him. He sure didn't look like he hated it if Rune was doing the fussing.

"Should you be up and about?" Rune asked, running his hands over Silas's abdomen. "Do you need help walking?"

"Yes," Silas said. "If you don't mind helping me." He leaned into the big man. "It's so hard to get around."

"Fucker almost hit me when I tried to help him down the shuttle stairs," Finn said, scowling at the two men.

"Hmm," Ma said. "I think you were just the wrong man offering help." Her eyes twinkled.

Right about then, Leti finally let Wyatt go. He turned to the group. "If you all aren't too tired, we're having dinner at our house. We'd love to spend some time with you all."

"Food," Dru said dreamily. "Cooked, yummy food."

"It's pitiful that nine adults won't cook anything more than instant dinners and MREs," Verion said.

"You only cook basic breakfast meals and grilled cheese, old man," Morgan said, pointing at him. "That's enough out of you."

"It's still better than the rest of you. No wonder every ship needs a cook," Verion said. They started through the gate. "Speaking of, where's Juniper? That man can cook."

WYATT CURLED up with Estella and Luna on a pile of

pillows and watched the slightly controlled chaos around him. They were all spread throughout Leti and Hack's spacious back yard. Ma, Juniper, and Lilah carried platters of food to a center picnic table. They darted around dogs, cats, and chickens. A goat nabbed an apple from the table and ran. Shit, there was also a pig. The pot-bellied pig waddled over and cuddled up to his side. What the hell?

"That's Porkchop. He's nice," Estella said sleepily. "All the people and animals are nice."

A large purple Grell ran about the yard in shifted form, chasing the kids, Wyatt's brothers included. "That's Grandpa Fasi," Estella said. "He's chasing Rizzie, Xu, and Nessa."

"That's the Lord Admiral?"

"Uh-huh. He likes to play with us," Estella said. "Where's Grandpa Very?"

"He's over there talking with Dru, Lerais, Hack, and Leti."

"Oh. Hack is holding Pepper. Isn't she cute?"

"She is," he answered. The baby's bright red hair shone in the sunlight, just like Leti's.

A little boy, around three years old, ran by with a large hunting cat at his side. A llama and another shifted Grell chased them. "That's Sami and his cat, Pax. Beck is the big wolfie. He's Uncle Hack's engineer. I like him a lot. The llama is Wobble. Have you ever seen a llama before?"

"I haven't," Wyatt said, watching in amazement. The llama and Grell worked in tandem to corner Sami and Pax.

A ten-foot-long Fire Veil Dragon walked past them. A large, fat rabbit rode on its back. "That's Princess Buttercup and Abbot."

"He's huge," Wyatt said. Fuck. What had they gotten into with Stardust?

"There's Mo," Estella said, pointing to a tall, skinny boy. He had already started in on the platters of food. "His brother, Alex, and his sister, Rose, are right over there." The older two sat with Morgan, Draif, and Lucas. They seemed enthralled with whatever nonsense the men were telling them.

Ma walked over to plop down beside them. She held Pela in her arms. "How are you two doing over here?"

"I'm telling him who everyone is," Estella said. "It's a bit overwhelming, I think."

"You are such a smart girl," Ma said. She leaned over and kissed Estella's head.

"I'm a lucky man to have her," Wyatt said in agreement. He watched Rune pamper Silas in a shaded corner of the yard. That would be fun to watch.

Pops carried a few plates balanced in his arms. "Love," he said, sending Ma a sweet look. "Food looks good." He handed her one of the plates. "Got you some too, son." He handed another to Wyatt. "Of course, I didn't forget our princess either." He handed the last to Estella.

"Thanks, Grandpops," the little girl said. "Granma and Juniper are the best cooks ever, Wyatt. You'll love it."

"I already do," he said, mouth full. A group of the

crew started up a card game by the buffet. Wyatt had to laugh when he saw Linc showing off Nugget to his hero, Dannol. Quinn seemed obsessed with following around a tiny, blonde woman.

"That's Cordy," Estella said, pointing out the blonde. "I heard Hazel say that Quinn loves her."

"Aww," he said and stuffed a roll in his mouth.

"Piggy," his mom said. Wyatt and Porkchop both gave her an affronted look. She handed him Kiki. "I need to go corral Jordan before he eats all of the food." Sure enough, Jordan was piling his plate high at the food table. His mom shook her head and jogged over.

"This is a good day," Wyatt said. He wished the older Kiki and Pela could have been there to see it all. They would have liked Charybdis Station. He held little Kiki close to his chest and thought about the Queen. She had been kind once. A good person. He felt bad for her. She likely would be horrified at what she had become.

He remembered a picture of her from Leti's presentation. She had stood in the middle of a battle, smiling and carrying a severed head. Now, she was a threat to the whole galaxy and would be pissed as hell about losing her lover.

She'd be angry to lose so many of her elements as well, but Water had needed to die and Death was his dad. Wyatt growled. The bitch could be as angry as she wanted. It wouldn't change a damn thing.

Leti suddenly started waddling across the yard. "Morgan! Is that a Frost Veil Dragon?"

"Oh, fuck," Hack said.

ALSO BY C.W. GRAY

The Blue Solace Series – science fiction/fantasy, mpreg

1. The Mercenary's Mate – https://amzn.to/2MAOFEH
2. The General's Mate – https://amzn.to/2G1abRE
3. The Soldier's Mate – https://amzn.to/2S7R6ng
4. The Lieutenant's Mate – https://amzn.to/2THZ47w
5. The Engineer's Mate – https://amzn.to/2HpI4vH
6. The Captain's Mate – https://amzn.to/2knP03W
7. The Rebel's Mate – *Coming Soon*
8. Fire's Mate – *Coming Soon*

The Hobson Hills Omegas – non-shifter, mpreg, omegaverse

1. Falling for the Omega – https://amzn.to/2BgWURV
2. Snow Kisses for My Omega – https://amzn.to/2TdDiol
3. Romancing the Omega – https://amzn.to/2UNENKD

4. Healing the Omega – https://amzn.to/2FNcXrY
5. A Pint for my Omega – https://amzn.to/2XItQf7
6. Unraveling the Omega – https://amzn.to/2xRCnRL
7. The Alpha's Christmas Wish – *Coming December 2019*

Hobson Hills Shorts – short stories from the world of Hobson Hills Omegas

1. The Beta's Love Song – https://amzn.to/2UrRPNN
2. Bennett's Dream – https://amzn.to/2GwSpG3
3. Justin's Journey – https://amzn.to/2DhW1t1
4. Grey's Gift – https://amzn.to/2BcjxXf
5. Hobson Hills Shorts: Volume One – https://amzn.to/2M3oGGZ

Holiday Omegas Shorts – holiday short stories from the world of The Silver Isles – paranormal, mpreg

1. Cauldron Cake Pops and a Witch's Kiss – https://amzn.to/33wMrhc
2. Sugar Cookies and a Witch's Love – *Coming December, 2019*
3. Candy Hearts and a Witch's Ring – *Coming in February, 2020*

The Silver Isles – paranormal, mermen, mpreg

1. The Guppy Prince
2. The Not so Little Merman – *Coming Soon*
3. The Sea Witch – *Coming Soon*

If you would like to keep up with releases, please like and follow me on Instagram (@c.w._gray) or Facebook (@cwgrayauthor), join C.W. Gray's Reading Nook on Facebook, or visit my website at https://cwgray-author.com.

Excerpt from *The Lieutenant's Mate* – Book Four in The Blue Solace

Anchor's Rest System, Charybdis Station

Sebastian Dolarnio kept his eyes closed, smiling softly. He was in his bed, wrapped up in soft sheets. A strong arm lay across his stomach, and he was pressed against a hard body. For the first time in a very long time, he was in bed with a man of his choice. His mate. His body was well-loved, not *used*. Alois' scent surrounded him, and Sebastian scooted back against him.

"Good morning, beautiful," Alois murmured against Sebastian's ear. He nibbled the pointed tip, sending a thread of heat through Sebastian's body. "I missed you so damn much."

"I missed you too," he said, rolling in his mate's arms. He cupped Alois' beautiful face. His sweet brown eyes were soft, and the red scales climbing up his neck tickled Sebastian's palms. His Dedril was a handsome man. "You had a job to do and Wyatt to rescue."

Sebastian knew the physical distance between the two of them for the past months had been for the best. It had given them time to talk and get to know one another without the issue of sex getting in the way. Sebastian *knew* Alois now. He knew he liked to appear like a silly, irresponsible, tomcat, but he wasn't like that at all. He was a bit silly, Sebastian thought with a smile, but he cared deeply about people and was deadly serious about serving Charybdis Station. He was a good man – a trustworthy man.

"I hate that I missed Nina's birth. I feel like I've already failed you and her," Alois said. He grumbled and turned his face to kiss Sebastian's palm.

"You would have just passed out if you had been here," Sebastian said, teasing. "We were fine. Leti and the rest of Blue Solace were there in your place."

"It's not the same," Alois said.

"I know," Sebastian said. He had wanted Alois there too. "If we ever have another baby, then we'll try to make sure you're there. Okay?"

"You're placating me," Alois said with a smile. He huffed out a breath. "Fine. We'll just have to have another baby to make sure it happens."

"Hold your horses there, buddy," Sebastian said. "Having babies hurts, and I'm only now able to have sex again. It's going to be a while." He hesitated. "You really didn't mind last night? I'll get better. I promise." Sebastian had thought he was beyond the fear he felt from his time on Union Station, but even with Alois, he hadn't been able to handle penetration.

Alois nodded and kissed him. His mouth tingled and he savored Alois' taste. "You went through a lot, beautiful. It'll take time to heal emotionally and mentally, but I'll be right here beside you."

"What if I can never handle sex?" Sebastian had wanted to be with Alois so badly last night, but he froze, filled with fear at the last second.

"There are a lot of ways to be intimate, beautiful. Remember last night?" Alois nuzzled his nose against

Sebastian's. "If you can never handle penetration, it's fine. You're my mate, and I'll treasure you always." Alois kissed him again. After ending the kiss, Alois gave him a mischievous look. "As for babies, if you insist, we'll wait two years. Our house has two extra bedrooms. That means two more babies, right?"

Nina's cries echoed through the baby monitor. "Why don't we worry about the baby we have?" Sebastian rolled out of bed, happy to see Alois hopping up too. They pulled on pants and went to the newborn's room.

Alois gently picked her up, cradling her in his arms. The light from the window lit up the room, making sparkles dance across her lavender skin. "She is so beautiful," Alois said in awe. "Look at those eyes. They're just like her papa's."

Sebastian stroked a finger across her cheek. "I never thought something so horrible could create someone so lovely." Her plump face scrunched up with another cry. "I think it's time for a fresh diaper and a bottle."

"I got this," Alois said confidently. "I've been practicing on Wyatt and Morgan's twins." He deftly changed the baby's wet diaper while Sebastian got her bottle ready. He handed it to his mate and watched him feed her. A deep satisfaction filled Sebastian at the sight. His man and his daughter. Alois shot him a look, smiling. "What do you want to do today? Our crew has the next two weeks off since the mission took so long."

"Hmm." Sebastian thought for a minute. "We could go to the trade market. I haven't managed to get there yet since I've been so busy with Leti."

"Have I mentioned how proud I am of you?" Alois leaned over and kissed his cheek. "You are so damn smart. I can't believe you, Leti, and Shae put everything together to figure out the artifact."

"You may have mentioned it a thousand or so times," Sebastian said, blushing. "All I did was translate things." He hadn't done much but everyone acted like he was a genius. "Leti and Shae did all the hard stuff." They had done the actual research, piecing together the story of the Queen and her elements. He wished he could have helped more, but he wasn't educated like Leti or incredibly smart like Shae.

"You don't give yourself enough credit," Alois said. "One day, you'll see in yourself what we all do. Then we'll all have fun telling you *I told you so*."

"If you say so," Sebastian said, shrugging. Alois and his friends didn't understand or were being too kind to see the truth. Alois was stuck with him now, though, so at least there was that. There would be no abandoning all hope once his mate actually realized who he was mated to.

Buy Here: https://amzn.to/2THZ47w

Excerpt from *Falling for the Omega*, Book One of the Hobson Hills Omegas

Carter loaded the last of his tools into his new work van and shut the door. His first day in his new profession was off to a good start. He had three clients to see today and eight spread out during the rest of the week.

Finally getting his plumbing license had been a good idea, even if his perfect, wealthy family hated the idea of him being a plumber.

Hell, they had also hated the idea of him being a soldier and of him moving out of state when he came back injured. They pretty much hated every decision he made.

The crisp fall wind was cold, but the gold, brown, and red leaves on the trees and ground made the cold worth dealing with. Autumn in Maine sure wasn't the same as autumn in Georgia, but so far, he was damn happy with the move. There was a peace here amongst the trees that he hadn't managed to find anywhere else.

"Hi, Mr. Neighbor!"

A child's voice came from behind him, startling Carter. He spun around, stumbling a bit on his prosthesis, and faced the little girl standing a few feet from his van.

She looked about five or six, with two black braids, caramel skin, and a freckled nose. When she smiled brightly, he saw a small gap between her two front teeth.

A black and gray miniature schnauzer sat at her feet, gaze stern and trained on him.

He looked around and didn't see any adults. His little half acre tract was quite a ways back from the road, nestled between a good-sized apple orchard on one side and a thick forest on the other.

Where the hell had this little girl come from?

"My name's Olive, and I brought you a welcome basket. I made it myself, but Daddy made you one too. He's gonna bring it tonight. I wanted you to get mine first, 'cause it's from me and then we'll be best friends." The little girl paused to take a breath. Her wide brown eyes sparkled and met his straight on, innocent and fearless. "We'll be best friends forever."

She didn't even seem to see the scars along the side of his face. The burn marks had already made two kids cry at the grocery store yesterday. Both times, the parents had been too embarrassed to apologize. They just grabbed their kids and ran.

"Uh, where's your daddy, Olive?" His voice was deep and cracked, broken by the scarring on his neck. Her adoring stare was starting to freak him out a little. He'd never really been around kids.

"He's at home," she answered and handed him the basket. "See what I brought you? Look, look, look."

"Do you know your phone number? Maybe we could give your daddy a call," Carter said, taking the basket from Olive. He pulled the small hand towel from the top and almost dropped the basket. "Is that a hedgehog?"

"Yep! That's Hodges the hedgehog. He wanted to

come visit too. Oh and this is Winston," she said and knelt to pet the small dog.

"Okay, your number?" He tried to keep his gruff voice kind. No sense in scaring the kid.

"Olive! Olive Persephone Wilson! Where are you?" A man's voice called from the orchard, full of panic and desperation.

"Uh oh," Olive said. She hurriedly looked around, then darted behind his van, Winston following her. "That's Daddy." She poked her head out and stared hard. "Tell. Him. Nothing."

She quickly hid again when a young omega rushed out of the orchard. He was her father, had to be. He looked just like her.

Carter suddenly couldn't catch his breath. The man in front of him was simply adorable. He was short and well formed, a little chubby. His black hair fell in curls around his face, and his wide hazel eyes contrasted beautifully with his caramel skin. The same freckles that decorated his daughter's nose, fell across his own. Where it looked cute on the kid, on her father... Bad thoughts, Carter! Bad thoughts!

"Have you seen a little girl? Black hair? Brown eyes? Miniature schnauzer with her? Maybe a hedgehog?"

Carter stared at the handsome man, mouth gaping, for too long.

The man frowned at him, tilting his head. "Are you alright?" His shy smile revealed the small gap between his front teeth.

Oh fuck, he was so damn perfect. He met Carter's eyes too, didn't even glance at the scars.

"Mister?"

Carter shook his head and did his best to pull himself together. He smiled, as best he could with the scar tissue, and nodded toward the van, holding a finger to his lips, encouraging the man to keep quiet.

Olive's father rolled his eyes and stomped around the van. A squealing Olive ran from her hiding spot and hid behind Carter, hugging him around the waist.

"Mr. Neighbor, save me!" Her giggling told him she wasn't too worried about her father catching her.

"Olive, you scared me to death running off like that." Her father really did look worried. "What have I told you about leaving the house without me?"

"But daddy," she whined. "I wanted to meet Mr. Neighbor. We're best friends now, and I gave him a welcome basket. I was being hospital."

Carter frowned. Hospital?

"Hospitable, baby girl, and it doesn't matter. You are too little to be wandering around by yourself and talking to strangers. No television time this week, and you have to clean out Pooka and Banjo's stalls on Saturday."

Olive gave a big sigh and leaned her forehead into Carter's leg. "Okay, Daddy, but it was worth it. I have a new best friend now."

The man met Carter's stare, a question in his eyes. Carter nodded and gave his best half smile.

"Well, maybe our new neighbor would like to come over for dinner one night? So that we can meet him properly," the man said.

"Yay! Mr. Neighbor, can you come tonight? Daddy's gonna make apple dumplins for dessert."

Carter smiled at the little girl and nodded. "Yeah, if it's okay with your dad."

The man smiled and nodded eagerly. "That would be great. I hardly ever get to cook for anyone but Olive." He gave a flustered look and held out his hand. "Oh, I forgot. My name is Elijah Wilson. I live in the farmhouse with the orchard. Of course, you've met Olive."

Carter shook his hand, touch lingering longer than it should. He was reluctant to release him but finally did. "Yeah, I'm Carter Benson. Just moved here from Georgia."

"Wow, so Maine's probably a bit different, huh?"

"Yeah, but all the colors on the trees? And ya'll actually have snow. I've never seen much of it."

"You say that like snow is a good thing." Elijah shuddered. "Well, welcome to Hobson Hill. I see Olive already gave you a welcome basket."

Carter looked back in it. "There's a hedgehog in there." His coarse voice was getting rougher as he spoke. He wasn't used to talking so much. Doctors said it was good for him to do though.

"I put cider in there for you. It's in my favorite big girl cup, the one with Moana. There's also butter from Pooka and some of Daddy's bread. It's so yummy!"

"Thanks, Olive. I appreciate it," Carter said. The little girl still hung on his leg, smiling up at him. She was a cute one, he acknowledged, even though she was clearly a little crazy. It was a good crazy though.

"Your alpha won't mind me coming," Carter asked Elijah.

The man winced and lowered his eyes. "I don't have an Alpha, so no, that won't be a problem."

Carter was surprised. Happy, but surprised. This adorable man had to be beating them off with a stick. Of course, some folks thought poorly about single omegas, and some alphas refused to even speak to them. Idiots.

"I guess I'll see you tonight. What time?"

"Oh, is six okay?" Elijah's confidence seemed to bounce back at Carter's question.

"That's fine. I better get to work."

"Yes, of course," Elijah said and pulled Olive off Carter's leg. "Come on, Olive. We better get back to the house. We need to get you to school."

"Okay. Bye, Carter, love you!" The little girl and her dog ran off through the orchard.

"I swear it's exhausting keeping up with her," Elijah sighed. Carter smiled and held the hedgehog out to him. "Thanks," he said, taking Hodges and smiling shyly. "See you tonight. Have a good day at work."

Carter stood frozen as he watched Elijah walk away. He was in trouble. Big, wonderful trouble.

Buy Here: https://amzn.to/2BgWURV

www.ingramcontent.com/pod-product-compliance
Lightning Source LLC
Chambersburg PA
CBHW071748190726
48292CB00003B/905